"KISS ME, THEN TELL ME IT'S OVER."

She struggled to her feet. "Forget it!"

Cas rose to join her. "What's the problem? If you're over what you felt for me, as you claim to be, then kissing me without emotion would prove it."

"This isn't a trial. I don't have to prove anything. And I never claimed that the physical attraction between us was dead."

"Then we'll begin with that."

Lisel opened her mouth to protest, but her words were stolen from her as he captured her parted lips. Cas gave her no chance for retreat. They were both breathless by the time his mouth left hers to voyage across her cheek. "Doesn't this tell you something?" he rasped.

"That I should stay away from you," she responded shakily. But it was a threat she knew she couldn't keep. . . .

CANDLELIGHT ECSTASY ROMANCES®

PRIVATE ACCOUNT

Cathie Linz

A CANDLELIGHT ECSTASY ROMANCE ®

Published by
Dell Publishing Co., Inc.
1 Dag Hammarskjold Plaza
New York, New York 10017

ISBN: 0-440-17072-9

Printed in the United States of America
First printing—June 1984

*In loving memory
of a
personal treasure—
my cat, Bit-Bit
1963–1983*

To Our Readers:

We have been delighted with your enthusiastic response to Candlelight Ecstasy Romances®, and we thank you for the interest you have shown in this exciting series.

In the upcoming months we will continue to present the distinctive sensuous love stories you have come to expect only from Ecstasy. We look forward to bringing you many more books from your favorite authors and also the very finest work from new authors of contemporary romantic fiction.

As always, we are striving to present the unique, absorbing love stories that you enjoy most—books that are more than ordinary romance.

Your suggestions and comments are always welcome. Please write to us at the address below.

Sincerely,

The Editors
Candlelight Romances
1 Dag Hammarskjold Plaza
New York, New York 10017

CHAPTER ONE

"Do . . . you . . . speak . . . English?" The words were drawn out and carefully enunciated by a deep male voice.

Lisel Mayer swiveled at the unexpected sound. She'd thought she was alone in the Austrian hotel; otherwise she would never have started humming "The Sound of Music." Rick always said she was tone-deaf. *Forget him,* she fiercely ordered. *What's done is done.*

"Do . . . you . . . speak . . . English?" The man repeated the question louder this time as if that might help her understand it.

"Yes." Lisel's reply was accompanied by an affirmative nod.

Before she could elaborate, he carefully asked, "Do you have a room?"

Now that was a touchy question. This late in the season, mid-September, the small hotel's owner accepted guests at his own discretion. But Siegfried had gone to Zell am See for the day, leaving Lisel in charge. Should she allow this man to stay or send him on his way? A ray of sunlight

11

shining in her eyes prevented her from getting a clear view of him.

The man, misinterpreting her silent deliberation for incomprehension, spoke again. Only this time it was more to himself than to her and was accompanied by a weary shrug of what promised to be broad shoulders. "This is obviously Mrs. Feinstein's way of getting even with me for not paying attention in her class."

After that inscrutable statement Lisel did indeed have serious doubts about having him stay. She was stepping forward, ready to tell him the hotel was closed, when she caught her first clear look at him. He had all the physical attributes she found attractive in a man, from the curly darkness of his head of healthy hair right down to the lean length of his powerful legs. She couldn't tell what color his eyes were, but they slanted downward at the outside corners and were fanned with laugh lines.

"Yes, we have a room," Lisel heard herself say.

She was rewarded with a warm smile. "Your English is very good," he told her, even though he'd heard her say only a handful of words. "Where did you learn it?"

A long-dormant streak of mischievousness made Lisel say, "Grade school."

"The schools here in Austria should be proud of you."

"I did not go to school here," she replied, her inflection deliberately precise.

"No? Where did you go to school?"

"Cleveland," she admitted with a grin.

The stranger surprised and delighted her by grinning in return. Finally! A man who could appreciate humor, even if it was somewhat at his own expense.

"You're an American?" the subject of her speculations asked.

Lisel nodded, her long braid of golden brown hair bobbing up and down in accompaniment.

"What are you doing here?"

Surely that was obvious, she thought with a disparaging glance down at her uniform. The black skirt and blouse with a white apron usually spoke for themselves. "I work here."

"Then I will definitely have to stay here for a while."

His eyes, she now realized, were brown, and they wandered over her face and body with a deliberateness that should have been offensive but wasn't. Lisel found herself returning the visual once-over. Inevitably their glances collided. Her blue-green irises reflected feminine appreciation while his gaze spoke of open admiration tinged with a lingering glint of laughter.

"Don't you want to see the rooms before you decide?" she questioned somewhat huskily.

"No. I've seen you."

Lisel couldn't help being flattered by the warmth of his voice. It singled her out, made her feel special. The feeling was reinforced by his continuing appraisal of her person.

Lisel tore herself away from his flirtatious spell-casting with difficulty, inviting her still-unnamed guest into the reception area. She reached behind the counter to gather up a registration form attached to a small clipboard. But instead of handing it to him, as was customary, she retained the clipboard in her possession and asked the questions aloud. "Your first name?" Her pencil was poised over the appropriate line.

"Cas."

Lisel dutifully recorded the information before continuing. "Surname?"

He told her. She tried guessing the spelling. "Is that C-A-L-E-N-S-K-I?"

"No." Cas moved closer until only the clipboard separated them.

Excited awareness scuttled through her bloodstream,

13

causing her eyes to widen perceptibly. Once again her glance was caught and held by his before both their eyes dropped to her wavering pencil.

"It's Kalensky with a *k* at the beginning and a *y* at the end." Cas managed to turn the simple spelling of his name into a softly spoken moment to be shared.

Lisel had to pause and readjust her breathing pattern to a more normal rate before going on to the next line. "Permanent address?"

He stepped back a pace, giving her more breathing room. "Twenty-nine West Walden Court, Chicago, Illinois."

"Six-oh-six-five-seven, right?" Lisel inserted.

"Don't tell me you've memorized the zip code book," Cas said mockingly.

"Nothing that impressive." She denied it with a laugh. "I happen to live a few blocks from Walden Court."

"I thought you said you were from Cleveland."

"I grew up in Cleveland," she corrected. "I haven't been back there since." Her pencil moved to the right. "Your birth date?"

"Three one fifty. And yours?"

Still trying to calculate his age, Lisel automatically answered, "Two three fifty-eight."

"That makes you what . . . twenty-six?"

She nodded, having figured out that he was thirty-four.

"Married, single, divorced?" she asked, even though that question wasn't actually on the form.

"Single."

Lisel couldn't help the slight smile that lifted the very corners of her expressive mouth. Looking up from her writing to see if Cas had noticed her reaction, she found him smiling at her in the manner of one sharing an intimate joke.

Bemused by the rapid velocity of her heartbeat, she

launched into her next inquiry. "Where did you come from?"

His eyes crinkled with mocking humor. "Are you asking for a biology lesson?"

She laughed and clarified her question. "I need to know your departure and destination points."

"Departure points? From the States?"

"No. Where you were last night."

"At what time?"

"Does it make a difference?"

"Yes. At six I was in a traffic jam on the German autobahn, but by eight I was in Austria. Nazareth, to be exact."

"You came from Nazareth?"

"Please." He held up a dismissing hand with teasing studiousness. "No religious questions."

"Nazareth was your departure point." She spoke her thought aloud as she wrote down the information. "Then where are you going after Fusch?"

"Fusch?"

"That's where you are now. Didn't you know?"

Cas shook his head. "All I knew was that I was too tired to undertake driving the Grossglockner Road today."

"Most people do drive right on through without stopping here," Lisel acknowledged. "At least during this time of year. This is the shoulder season."

He eyed her appreciatively. "And nice shoulders they are, too."

She returned the compliment. "I have to say that the feeling is mutual." Her pencil wandered right off the clipboard. "Umm." She cleared her throat before asking, "Where are you headed from here?"

" 'Who knows what tomorrow brings?' " he quoted from a popular song.

15

Lisel left that section blank and handed Cas the clipboard so that he could sign the bottom of the form.

"One more thing," she added. "Who's Mrs. Feinstein?"

"My high school German teacher." He returned the clipboard to her. "Okay, now it's my turn." After whipping what looked like a business card out of his wallet, he snatched her pencil. "Name?"

"Lisel."

"Nice," he said complimentarily. "Surname?"

"Mayer with an *a* and an *e*."

"Birth date I already know. Two three fifty-eight."

"You've got a good memory."

"That's not all I've got," he murmured, his overstated lechery making Lisel laugh. "But more about that later." He briskly resumed his interrogation. "For now back to the questions. Married, single, divorced?"

"Single."

This time he was guilty of the same half smile Lisel had displayed earlier. "What's your favorite color?" he improvised, expanding the line of questioning.

"Purple."

"Mine's red," Cas told her. "You forgot to ask."

"There wasn't enough space on the form," she said.

"That's no excuse. Favorite food?"

"Chocolate."

"Favorite song?"

Lisel's eyes reflected more green than blue, a sure sign of impending mischievousness. " 'Pachelbel Canon.' "

"You expect me to fit that on the back of this tiny card?"

"Would you like me to spell it out for you?"

"No, thank you. Some things don't have to be spelled out." His gaze rested on her mouth, noting the smile lifting her lips. "Besides, that's one of my favorite songs, too."

16

"It is?"

"Even before it was used in the movie *Ordinary People*. But actually I have a hard time choosing between that and another piece of music."

"Oh? What's that?"

" 'Jailhouse Rock,' " he replied with a perfectly straight face.

Lisel's smile widened into a grin. "I think it would be safe to say that you must be a man of diverse tastes."

"I'd love to talk to you in more detail about my . . . tastes. When do you get off?"

"It's not as simple as that." Lisel had no set hours, especially now that the summer season was over. In fact, these next two weeks were something of a vacation for her.

"What's complicating matters? I thought you might take pity on a fellow countryman and show me around."

"I think you already know your way around," she dryly replied.

"Oh, I do," he softly assured her. "In most areas. But not around the Austrian Alps."

"Then we'll have to supplement your education, Mr. Kalensky."

"Call me Cas. Since you're going to be my personal guide, I think we should be on a first-name basis, don't you, Lisel?"

She nodded, strangely gratified by the way he said her name. It was almost as if she'd been waiting a lifetime for someone to say "Lisel" in just that way. *Get a hold on yourself,* she sternly instructed herself. *It's harmless enough to flirt with this guy, but don't go overboard.*

"Let me show you to your room," she briskly stated.

As Cas followed her up the wide marble staircase, he didn't notice the delicate watercolors of local wild flowers displayed on the whitewashed walls. Instead his attention

17

was focused on the tanned firmness of Lisel's shapely legs as she climbed the stairs in front of him.

Lisel knew he was staring at her because she felt a telltale prickle along the back of her neck. By waiting for him on the landing, she made certain that their ascent up the remainder of the steps was made side by side. But having him beside her was no better than having him behind her, for now she felt more than a telltale prickle. Now there was the accidental brushing of elbows, the slightest whiff of his citrus aftershave, the sudden realization of his height.

Their glances ricocheted like awkward children's. Yet there was nothing childlike about the way Lisel felt, nothing childlike about the unmistakable interest Cas displayed. This was a decidedly adult form of anticipation!

"How long will you be staying with us?" Lisel asked as she opened room 102.

"I had originally planned on staying only a night or two," Cas replied from close beside her. "But I now find this place too tempting to leave."

"I'm glad," she softly murmured before more firmly tacking on, "that you like the room, that is. There's a lovely view." She threw back the curtains to display an Alpine scene that could have been lifted right off a calendar.

Cas strolled over to admire the view, but his attention soon came back to rest on her. "Very beautiful."

"You like what you see?" she heard herself asking with flirtatious lightness, wondering at the effect this man had on her metabolism.

Cas indirectly answered her question by saying, "The beauty is so close I can almost reach out and touch it."

Lisel held her breath, waiting for his actions to match his words. She was not disappointed.

The very tip of his index finger softly brushed across her cheek. "Smudge," he explained with a knavish grin.

"Thank you." Her face tingled from the momentary contact.

"Anytime."

"Speaking of time, when would you like your breakfast in the morning? It's included in the price of the room."

"Breakfast in bed?" The teasing note in his voice prevented her from taking offense.

She shook her head, her braid sliding around her shoulder. "Breakfast in the dining room downstairs. We normally serve from seven thirty until nine thirty, but since you're our only guest—"

"I am?" Cas looked pleased at the news.

"At the moment, so it would help if you told us what time you'd like breakfast."

"Nine would be fine."

"I guess that's everything then. The room has its own private bathroom." She pointed to a door across from the bed. "There are towels hanging on the racks."

"Fine."

"These are your keys. The large one opens the front door; the smaller one is for your room."

He took her hand in his, keys and all, narrowing the space between them. "Lisel . . ."

There it was again, that tug on her heartstrings at the sound of her name on his lips. "Yes." It was meant to be a question, but her shallow breathing made it sound like a husky supplication.

Caught by an invisible lasso, she swayed nearer. The minty freshness of his breath swirled across her skin in a tantalizing prelude of things to come.

"Lisel." Cas repeated her name, the sound of it reverberating against her mouth.

A second later her name was called yet again, but this

time it was bellowed in a yodeler's voice and the sound reverberated up the stairs. "Lisel!"

She drew away. "I'd better go."

Cas's protest was drowned out by the yodeler's second "Lisel!"

"He'll come up here looking for me," she warned. "I've got to go."

"Who is he?"

"Siegfried Mayer."

"Mayer?" Cas questioned sharply. "With an *a* and an *e*?"

"Yes."

"You told me you weren't married." His look was accusatory.

"You really should learn not to jump to conclusions. Remember where that got you with me."

"I haven't gotten anywhere with you yet," he retaliated with a return of his humor. "But we'll go into that later. For now just tell me who Siegfried is."

Before Lisel could speak, a brawny blond giant entered the room, issuing a booming greeting in German.

"Our guest doesn't understand German," Lisel explained in that language.

"Guest?" Siegfried questioned, also in German since he hated speaking English.

"He's an American. I thought you wouldn't mind his staying."

"American? We don't get many of them stopping here."

"What's he saying?" Cas demanded of Lisel.

"Siggy was just saying that we don't get many Americans staying here."

"Don't tell me *Siggy*," he mockingly mimicked, "doesn't like Americans!"

"Of course not. Look at me. I'm an American and

20

. . ." She trailed off, realizing how the rest of her statement could be misinterpreted.

It made no difference. Cas completed it for her. ". . . he likes you. Yes, but you would appeal to him in ways I don't."

"Siegfried is the owner of this hotel. He's also my cousin."

"Cousin?" Cas now showed signs of discomfiture.

"That's right. Cousin," she defined, "as in father's brother's son."

Another burst of German directed Lisel's attention back to Siegfried. "Why did you allow him to stay?" her cousin was demanding. "You know we are almost ready to close."

Lisel could hardly say that a pair of hooded brown eyes and a pair of broad shoulders had swayed her decision, so she improvised. "If he'd wanted to stay only one night, I would have said no. But he wants to stay several days, and I thought even one guest was better than no guests at all this week. After all, we aren't closed yet."

"Now you sound like Maria," Siegfried said, referring to his wife, who was in Salzburg for the day.

Cas watched the verbal interchange with narrowed eyes. The rapid idioms Lisel and her cousin were speaking had very little resemblance to the few halting phrases he remembered from his freshman high school German class.

Lisel finished speaking to Siegfried and turned to face Cas. "Siegfried wanted to know if you needed any help with your luggage."

"No. Thank you." The latter Cas directed toward Lisel's cousin. "I can bring it up myself. In fact, I'll do that right now."

Only when Cas stepped outside did he realize that the clear skies had turned gray and were discharging a steady rainfall, which forced him to sprint to his rental car. By the time he walked in the hotel's front door with his suitcase his jacket was soaked and his hair was dripping water into his eyes.

Lisel was there to greet him upon his entrance into the small foyer. Noting the way his curly hair lay plastered against his head, giving him the endearing appearance of a wet puppy, she said, "It looks like you ran into one of those showery spells the forecasters were predicting."

"I've run into some kind of spell," he said teasingly.

"Is it too dampening for you?" she challenged.

"Not in the least." He paused to make sure she'd received the message before admitting, "I don't relish going out in that downpour again to find a restaurant for dinner."

"I suppose you could eat in the dining room here," she reflected. "It wouldn't be anything fancy, just *wiener schnitzel* and *pommes frites.*"

"I think I can manage to translate that, and it sounds delicious to me."

"Dinner will be served in the dining room in forty minutes."

"Great. That gives me enough time to take a warm shower."

"It looks to me like you've already had a shower," she said, teasing him.

"Ah, but it doesn't count if you're fully clothed."

"I seem to have heard that line before," she scoffed.

"Is that right? You'll have to tell me all about it over dinner. See you then!"

Cas was gone before she could explain that she wouldn't be having dinner with him. She, Siggy, Maria, and their two children ate in the kitchen while the guests ate in the dining room with its traditional Tyrolean interior. Besides, she wasn't suitably dressed to eat dinner with him.

22

Basic black may be in this year, but not teamed with a frilly white apron!

Cas was already seated and waiting when Lisel came into the dining room forty minutes later. She'd meant to change, but Maria had gotten home late from Salzburg and needed an extra pair of hands in the kitchen. Lisel was now intent on carrying the platter containing Cas's dinner. After depositing it on the table before him, she removed the silver cover with a flourish.

"Looks good," he complimented, looking at her instead of the food, for Lisel's face wore an adorable look of concentration, complete with pearly white teeth worrying her lower lip, while she set about transferring the decoratively displayed food from the platter to his plate.

When she'd finished, without so much as dropping one french fry, she proudly said, *"Bon appetit!"*

"Where's your plate?" Cas demanded, handcuffing her wrist with lean fingers.

"In the kitchen."

"It's lonely out here by myself. Won't you join me?"

Her pulse raced beneath his gently restraining fingers.

"You'd be doing me a big favor." He pressed home his advantage.

She gave him an inquiring look.

"I can't eat all this food myself," he explained. "I'd get fat."

Her gaze slipped over his masculine frame, searching for any sign of flab. She found none. What she did find were lean muscles sheathed by the close fit of his red flannel shirt and jeans. "You look all right to me," she had to say.

"That's only because this is the beginning of my vacation. If I'm expected to eat this much every day"—he waved a hand at his loaded plate—"I'll have to be rolled

23

onto the plane to get home. You wouldn't want to do that to me, now would you?"

Numerous thoughts of what she would like to do to him occurred to her!

"You're taking an awful long time to answer my question," Cas prompted.

"I was thinking."

"Imagining me being rolled onto the seven forty-seven?"

"Something like that," she said tantalizingly.

"And?"

"And I will join you for dinner." She added another plate and silverware from the sideboard and slid into the seat across the table from him.

Reaching for the salt, Cas said, "So tell me, Lisel Mayer, what are you doing here in the middle of Austria?"

Lisel helped herself to a small portion of potatoes and a piece of golden brown breaded veal before replying, "I already told you all about myself."

"You haven't told me why you're here."

"To prevent you from having to be rolled onto a seven forty-seven, remember?"

"Ahah! Now we're getting somewhere!"

"We are?"

"I certainly hope so," he lowered his voice to murmur. "I've been searching half my life for you, and I'm not about to lose you after a shared platter of *wiener schnitzel!*"

"I see. You're waiting until we've shared dessert, is that it?"

"That's one way of putting it."

Lisel met his gaze full on, not coquettishly lowering or even fluttering her lashes. Their silent communication continued. Then, as if the emotional buildup were too intense, their eyes slid apart.

24

Lisel spoke first. "I'm polishing my accent."

"Is that what you'd call it?" Cas muttered, half to himself.

"You asked me what I was doing here in the middle of Austria," she reminded him, "and I'm telling you."

"Does that mean your occupation is not that of a full-time hotel worker?" he formally inquired.

"It is not," she confirmed, taking another bite of veal.

"Guess that cuts down on my chances of room service, huh?" He shot her a teasing look before asking, "What do you do for a living?"

"I'm an interpreter. That is, I soon will be," she revised. "I've got a job waiting for me in Chicago."

"Why are you over here if you've got a job waiting for you in Chicago?"

"The person presently in the position doesn't retire until October first. I was interviewed for the job last spring and told I'd been selected after I got my degree in June. When the opportunity arose for me to help Siggy here in Fusch for the summer, it seemed the ideal opportunity for me to perfect an Austrian accent."

"Isn't German the same all over?"

"Not at all. The accents vary as much in German as they do in English. A Cockney accent in England sounds completely different from a Texas drawl. And an Austrian accent sounds different from a Swiss. Even within Germany itself the accents vary widely from north to south." Aware that she'd been babbling on, she quickly changed the subject. "Now how about telling me about yourself?"

"Me? I'm just your average American tourist out to see the sights."

"You don't look like a typical tourist," she mused, crunching on a crispy french fry.

"Oh? Why's that?"

25

"You don't have a camera hanging around your neck. And your shirt isn't garish enough. Try again."

"Actually I'm an economist."

Lisel shook her head. "You don't look like an economist either."

"How should an economist look?"

"Tweedy," she answered. "You seem more denimy."

"Is that good or bad?"

Her voice was alive with amusement. "On you it looks good."

"How kind of you to notice," he replied in falsely modest tones. "I have only one question to ask."

"Yes?" She nibbled on another french fry.

"What are you doing for the rest of your life?"

CHAPTER TWO

The french fry Lisel was nibbling went down the wrong way, causing her to sputter and grab for her glass of water.

Once he'd assured himself that she wasn't in danger of choking, Cas said, "If that question is too hard to answer, let's narrow it down. What are you doing tomorrow?"

"I'm not sure," she cautiously replied.

"That's not the right answer," he chastised. "You're supposed to say that you're taking me sight-seeing tomorrow."

She set her water glass down. "I am?"

Cas viewed her reproachfully. "Don't you remember agreeing to be my guide?"

"Can't say that I do."

"Does that mean that I have to ask you all over again?" he asked in a show of male resignation that came complete with a heavy sigh.

"Guess it does," she maintained.

"In that case . . ." He put down his fork and took her hand in his. "Lisel Mayer, would you do me the great honor of acting as my guide?"

27

As before, her senses were keenly attuned to his touch. Trying to make light of the situation, she kidded, "Since you ask so politely, how can I refuse?"

"Does that mean the answer is yes?"

She nodded, sending the length of her golden braid into motion. "The answer is yes."

His hold on her hand grew more intimate as his thumb stroked the heart of her palm. "I'm glad." His voice alone was a caress.

Lisel was uneasily aware of the powerful attraction between them. It was there in the warmth of his touch—a warmth that traveled up her arm and spread throughout her system. Warning signals flashed, reminding her of what had gone wrong in her past and cautioning her not to let history repeat itself.

"Am I making you feel uncomfortable?" Cas astutely questioned, registering her slight stiffening.

"Yes," she baldly stated.

"Why?" Reluctantly releasing her hand, he held her pinned by his direct gaze.

She shifted uncomfortably before launching into speech. "Look, I don't want to seem presumptuous, but I can't afford an . . . involvement right now."

His voice reached out to her. "Care to tell me about it?"

"About what?" she hedged.

"About the guy who put that unhappy look in your eyes."

"Suffice it to say that I've recently ended a relationship."

He caught the bitterness hidden in her clipped inflection. "I take it you didn't part the best of friends?"

She and Rick, friends? "Hardly."

"What went wrong?"

"You certainly get right to the point, don't you?" she noted with an element of irritation.

His lips lifted in a beguiling smile. "It's all right. You can confide in me."

Strangely enough Lisel did feel that she could confide in Cas. "It's a very long and complicated story that boils down to one very simple fact." She paused, caught up in old memories.

"Which is?" Cas prompted.

"Rick may have loved me, but he never liked me." The words held a stark realization that had nothing to do with self-pity.

Muttering an expletive under his breath, Cas bluntly and succinctly stated, "Then he's an idiot!"

"Thanks," she acknowledged with a smile that reached all the way to the green flecks in her otherwise blue eyes. "I needed that."

"Friends?" He held out his hand.

She took it. "Friends."

"Good." His handshake was firm and decisive. "Now where are we off to tomorrow? You can take the day off, can't you?"

"No problem. This next week is my last in Austria, and I was planning on using it as a sort of minivacation anyway."

"Then it was very fortunate for both of us that I came along when I did."

"Indubitably." She agreed in a teasing drawl.

"Where should we begin?"

Had his emphasis on the word "begin" been deliberate? mocking provocation? She checked his face for corroborating evidence but found only congenial interest. Mentally chastising her overactive imagination, she asked, "Have you ever been to this area before?"

Cas shook his head.

"Then the wisest thing would be to begin with Zell am See," she decided. "Are you through with your dinner?"

"Yes, thanks. It was delicious."

Lisel was efficiently stacking their plates on a tray as she replied, "I'll tell Maria you liked it."

"Maria?"

"Siggy's wife."

Cas looked very pleased at the news. "So he's married, huh?"

"With two kids."

His smile faded when he saw her struggling with the laden tray. "Here, let me carry that."

"You can't!"

"Don't be ridiculous. Of course I can." He took the tray from her and mocked. "Did you think it was too heavy for me?"

"I didn't mean that you wouldn't be *able* to carry it. I meant that you're a guest and *shouldn't* be carrying it."

Cas ignored her attempts to regain possession of the tray's handles. "Are we going to stand here arguing about it or are you going to hold the kitchen door open for me?"

"I thought we'd stand here arguing about it," she couldn't resist answering.

"That'll teach me to ask." He headed toward the door.

"Where are you going?"

"To the kitchen."

"That door leads to the storage room. The one on your left leads to the kitchen."

"Thanks," he said in a droll voice.

"I didn't realize you'd need the assistance of a guide *within* the hotel," she teased.

He returned to her side. "Just for that you can have your tray back!"

She cracked up at the devilish humor she saw displayed in his dark eyes. "That's all right. You keep it," she generously allowed.

"Then open the kitchen door." His growl was more mirth-provoking than menacing.

"Yes, sir!" She hurried to the door and briskly held it open. "Anything to please a guest."

"Anything?" He leered as he went by.

"Almost anything," she revised.

Cas placed the tray on the cleared expanse of a countertop. "There! Now you've got no excuse not to join me in the other room."

Their return to the dining room was marked by the sound of music.

"It must be eight o'clock." Lisel smiled and rubbed her hands up and down her arms, smoothing out the goose bumps that never failed to appear no matter how often she heard this melody. Music had always had the power to move her deeply, another trait Rick hadn't appreciated.

"What does the music have to do with the time?" Cas's face reflected his puzzlement. "Unless you have a musical cuckoo clock?"

Lisel laughed and shook her head, "Maria gives the kids zither lessons at eight each evening, like clockwork. The family's quarters run adjacent to the kitchen. That's why you can hear them so well."

Tilting his head, Cas listened to the unique sound of the stringed musical instrument before pronouncing, "I like it. Makes me feel like I should expect Julie Andrews to come waltzing in."

"*The Sound of Music* was filmed northeast of here, near Salzburg."

"I've never heard this tune before."

"It's something they're practicing for a local festival. Maria is very much into her traditional heritage. She's a very talented artist and did all the watercolors displayed throughout the hotel. In fact, she's one of the few artists

31

in the country who know the delicate art of painting on spider webs."

"You've got to be kidding!"

"I'm not. There's an example on that wall over there."

Cas strolled over to admire the delicate workmanship. "Your family is very talented."

Lisel went on, proudly relating some more of their accomplishments. One thing led to another, and their conversation turned to all sorts of subjects: from tastes in music to the problems of the recession. Time passed unnoticed, and both were amazed at the number of things they had in common.

It was raining when they eventually said their good nights in the hallway, and it was still drizzling the next morning as they strolled through the old town center of Zell am See. Here the streets were too narrow to allow cars, small though the European models were. The rain sent them inside more shops than they would have ordinarily visited. Cas looked at everything but only bought an English-edition newspaper.

Since she was in town, Lisel took the opportunity to place an order for individual cream pitchers that Maria wanted for the hotel. The specialty store had four stories, and the special order department was on the top floor. Cas strolled around while Lisel placed Maria's order. She'd just finished the business transaction when Cas returned to her side.

"Come over here, I've got something to show you!" He grabbed hold of her hand and hurriedly guided her through the expensive displays of glassware. Stopping in front of a row of wineglasses, he admiringly exclaimed, "There!"

"Very nice," she said politely, even though she saw nothing in the plain stemware to warrant such enthusiasm.

32

Confused by her courteous but lackluster response, Cas followed her gaze. "No, not the glasses!" he exclaimed. "Look out the window!"

She did so and caught her breath at the double rainbow she saw hovering over the lake. "Come on!" It was her turn to grab his hand. "Let's go!"

"Go where?" he asked as they hurried down the stairs.

"To the end of the rainbow," she replied between pants, directing all her energy into bolting down the stairs.

"Yes, Dorothy," he said in mock acquiescence. Once they reached the store's street-level door, Cas held it open for her and asked teasingly, "Are we off to see the Wizard?"

Lisel grinned in return. "Who knows what we'll find there?"

They tried keeping their eyes peeled on the rainbow, which made dodging between the passing pedestrians rather difficult. Luckily they were only two blocks away from the lake, so not much damage could be done.

"What efficiency!" Cas marveled. "There's even a sign pointing to it."

"Where?"

"Right over there. The one that just says 'See' and an arrow."

" 'See' is pronounced *zay* in German, and it means 'lake.' "

"So Zell am See . . ."

". . . means Zell on the lake," she completed. "Oh, look! The rainbow's still here!"

Indeed it was, and it ended right in the middle of the lake.

They watched the twin set of rainbows fade away as the sunshine took hold and banished the remaining rain clouds to the surrounding mountain peaks.

"While we're down here . . ." She trailed off, rummaging in her large shoulder bag for something.

"What are you looking for?"

"This!" Lisel triumphantly held a small paper bag aloft. After opening it, she pulled out a hard roll and made her confession. "I snitched a few from the breakfast table."

"What for?"

"For the ducks." She shredded the roll and tossed bits down to the gabbling birds.

"How about the swans?" he asked.

"What swans?"

"The ones headed this way at full speed."

Sure enough the feathered flotilla she was feeding soon included two graceful but greedy swans.

"Here, help me," Lisel implored as the more aggressive of the two swans almost bit her finger in its haste to taste some bread. She handed Cas two rolls of his own. "You feed them, too."

"Ah, 'A Jug of Wine, a Loaf of Bread—and Thou.' . . ."

"We don't have any wine," she pointed out.

"Two out of three ain't bad."

"And I'm not sure that *Brötchen* qualifies as a loaf of bread either."

"Picky, picky," he scolded, directing a well-aimed bit of dough to a shy duckling swimming on the fringes of the crowd. After carefully distributing the rest of his *Brötchen,* he asked, "Are you ready to go?"

"Just give me a minute to tie my shoe." Lisel sat down on the low brick parapet fronting the lake and lifted her right foot. In less than her allotted minute she stood up again, shaking the few remaining bread crumbs from her fingers before dusting off the seat of her jeans. Only then was she aware that something was amiss. Her fingers came into contact with cold metal. Imitating the swans she'd

34

just been feeding, Lisel swiveled her head over her shoulder in an attempt to see what she'd felt.

"Something wrong?" Cas inquired.

"Yes."

"What is it?"

Color rushed into her face as she finally identified the problem. "I seem to have sat on a fishhook," she realized in a small voice.

"You're kidding!" He eyed her discomfited face before putting a hand on her shoulder and turning her around. Checking her pert posterior, he said, "You're not kidding. Okay, now just stand still." His hand released her shoulder and lowered. . . .

"What are you going to do?" It was more an exclamation than a question.

"Help you." His fingers carefully ran over her denim-clad bottom.

"Not here." She grabbed his arm, frantically indicating their public surroundings. A few yards away a group of children were taking their turn at feeding the ducks while two elderly women indulgently looked on.

"You can't walk," Cas patiently explained. "The hook will only dig into your skin." Another thought occurred to him. "When was the last time you had a tetanus shot?"

"A few months ago."

His brows lifted inquiringly. "Don't tell me you make a habit of this?"

"Very funny." She glared. "It wasn't a fishhook that time; it was a nail."

"You sat on a nail?"

"No, I cut my hand on one. But the fishhook is only caught on the jeans, not on me."

"At least not yet," he qualified.

Lisel stubbornly made no comment while the group of

35

children ran farther along the lake, out of sight. The two women hastily followed suit.

"Look, the coast is clear now," Cas declared. "There's no one around. Why don't we try to, er, disengage that nasty-looking weapon now?"

"How do you propose we do that?"

"You stand there, and I'll bend down here"—the direction of his voice moved downward from above her shoulder to near her waist—"and survey the situation."

Her eyes flickered from side to side, checking for intruders on this embarrassing scene. "Be careful," she warned.

His fingers stilled. "Did I hurt you?"

"No, but these are my best pair of jeans. Don't ruin them."

"I'll do my best, ma'am," he drawled. Standing up again, he said, "Maybe you'd better unfasten your Calvins."

"What!"

"I am not going to take indecent liberties." His teasing inflection then turned serious. "That fishhook really has the potential to hurt you. It's one of those four-pronged things that are designed to kill."

"Kill a trout, maybe. Not me."

"Would you rather injure yourself and have a doctor stitch you up?" Cas bluntly demanded.

"No," she shakily replied. Lisel avoided both doctors and dentists like the plague.

"Then undo your pants. You can pull your jacket down in the front if that will satisfy your modesty. And you'd better pull out my copy of the *Herald Tribune* that you offered to carry."

"This is no time to read a newspaper," she hissed.

"I'm not going to read it. . . ." He muttered something better left unsaid. "Look, do you want to stand here argu-

36

ing or do you want me to help you?" The look on her face answered his question. "Then give me the paper."

She did so.

"Okay, now the first thing I'm going to do is slide the *Trib* in between you and your Calvins." His manner was calm, like that of a physician explaining an operation. "That way I won't have to worry about hurting you while I'm working on this." Easing the denim material away from her waist, he made no comment about the generous glimpse he got of her sassy hot pink bikini underwear.

Lisel could feel his hands competently working to free the hook. She was grateful that Cas didn't take advantage of her misfortune. His touch didn't become more intimately familiar than the job required. Even so, she still felt its impact.

Her pulse was surging alarmingly by the time he finally declared, "Done." Her heart rate increased further when his fingertips accidentally brushed against the base of her spine while removing the newspaper. Shivers chased their way across her skin.

Cas's voice sounded rather thick as he said, "It's safe to refasten everything now."

Lisel simultaneously worked on redoing her jeans and reducing her pulse. Once both her clothing and her responses were under control, she turned and asked, "Is that what caused all the trouble?" indicating the lethal-looking hook.

"You were lucky not to have been hurt!" The thickness in his voice had been replaced by a blistering anger. "I'd like to get my hands on the idiot that left this thing lying around!"

"What are you going to do with it?" she asked, shivering from his rage even though it was not directed at her.

"Dispose of it as it should have been in the beginning." He strode over to a metal waste container and dropped the

37

fishhook in. "There, that's taken care of. Now, how are you?"

"Me? I'm fine." Hoping to lighten the situation, she asked, "How are my jeans?" She ran her hands over the smooth denim, searching for a rip.

"Your jeans are fine," he assured her, a grin lightening his features. "I meant to tell you earlier that they do wonders for your long legs."

"Thanks. And thanks for freeing me from the fishhook."

His right brow lifted, creating a look of roguish anticipation. "Don't you think a little reward might be called for?"

As she moved closer, her hands slid up to the unzippered V of his waterproof jacket. Without further ado Lisel placed a swift kiss on his lips. They were firm and warm; that much she noticed before quickly stepping away.

"That wasn't so difficult, was it?" he softly queried.

"No, it wasn't difficult," she acknowledged, surprised by the discovery.

"You may even grow to like it!" he suggested hopefully, his eyes taking on a devilish gleam.

"That is within the realm of possibility, I suppose." Her show of musing doubtfulness was intentional, right down to the absent tapping of her fingertip against her lips.

"Don't overwhelm me with your enthusiasm," Cas drawled.

"I'll try to restrain myself," she teasingly drawled in return. Checking her watch, she added, "We'd better get back to the car; our parking meter will be in the red."

"We haven't eaten lunch yet, you know."

"Oh!" She momentarily pressed her hand to her mouth at the oversight. "That's right, we didn't eat."

"You were too busy feeding the ducks."

"We have to feed the meter before we can feed ourselves," she reminded him.

Fortunately they arrived at their parking space before a meter maid did. "What does it eat?" Cas asked, indicating the elapsed meter.

"Schillings."

He pulled a handful of change from the front pocket of his jeans, tossing her a quizzical glance. "I thought that schillings were English currency."

"Used to be. England uses pounds and pence now."

He directed his attention toward his palmful of change. "Okay, which one of these do I feed it?"

"A few of these." She plucked out several copper-colored coins and inserted them into the meter. "Okay, now let's go eat."

But it wasn't that easy because they'd passed the serving hours for lunch and the restaurants were no longer open.

"I think it would be better if we picked up some fruit and cheese from a grocery store," Lisel suggested. "The sun's out now, so we could drive to a scenic spot and have a picnic. What do you think?"

"Cheese and fruit?" Cas looked dismayed. "I haven't had anything since breakfast, and that was only rolls and coffee."

"We could always add some dessert to our fruit and cheese." Her face lit up at her suggestion.

"I saw you eyeing those bakeries we passed." His accusation was tempered by a teasing smile.

"I did tell you that chocolate is my favorite food."

"So you did. I think you planned this."

"Planned it!"

Cas nodded emphatically. "Planned it so we'd miss lunch and have to eat chocolate."

"You may be right." She grinned.

A short while later, with apples and cheese already

39

purchased, they stood in front of a *Konditorei's* glass case displaying numerous gastronomical delights. "What would you like?" Lisel asked Cas while they waited for their number to be called.

"You really want to know?" he bent down to ask with a wicked intonation.

Lisel refused to show how much the soft tickling of his breath against her ear had affected her. Instead she firmly countered with "Only if what you want is inside this glass case."

"What would you recommend?"

"Being a chocolate lover, the *Sachertorte* is one of my favorites."

He searched the assortment of pastries before him. "Which one is that?"

"The one with a solid chocolate top and no frosting. Or you could try the chocolate torte that has four layers with chocolate icing between each one. The Florentine is also good. That has whipped cream, custard, and jam in between flaky layers of pastry. Then there's mocha or hazelnut; both of those are delicious."

"Thanks." He eyed her enthusiastic face with indulgent mockery. "You're a big help. You've recommended everything."

"Well? What are you going to order?"

"The *Sachertorte.* And you?"

"The chocolate torte." Lisel reached in her shoulder bag for her wallet.

"It's my treat," Cas firmly stated, dropping her wallet back in the bag. "Look on it as a means of my paying you back for this morning's city tour."

"Had I known you were going to pay me with chocolate I would have agreed to be your guide much sooner," she impishly stated.

Before Cas could retaliate, Lisel had turned to speak

40

with the shopkeeper, conversing in a rapid-fire German that was unintelligible to Cas. Only when it came to paying the bill was he able to comprehend what was going on. Cash registers spoke a certain universal language all their own!

"Okay, where to now?" Cas asked as he tucked his wallet back inside the inner pocket of his jacket.

"To a park bench I know of." At his confused frown she added, "It has one of the best views around."

"Is it within walking distance?"

"No, it's a short drive away."

"It had better be a *real* short drive or your driver may faint from hunger."

Cas did not faint before they reached their destination. "Well? Was it worth it?" Lisel demanded, waving her hand in a sweeping inclusion of the surrounding landscape. The bench they were sitting on had a front-row view of the Hohe Tauern range. The late-afternoon sun had swept off all remainders of the earlier rainsqualls, and a calm splendor overspread the mountains, softening the harshness of their outlines without distracting from their strength. Green pastures, dotted with chalets and covered with cows, were spread out before them.

"Definitely."

"What made you choose the Alps as a vacation site?" Lisel asked in between bites of her apple.

"I wanted to get away from things."

He sounded so grim that Lisel felt compelled to ask, "What things?"

"Just things," he dismissed. "I also wanted to come see if the Alps were as beautiful as I'd heard."

"And? Are they?"

"Even more so. There's a sort of rejuvenating peace here that allows you to recharge your batteries. This is a world away from the constant throb of Chicago."

"You said you were an economist. Where do you work in Chicago?" Her question was voiced to the accompaniment of distant cowbells.

He named one of the city's largest banks.

"You're a banker?" She tossed her apple core into the bag and tossed Cas a challenging grin. "Then what are you doing renting an Opel Kadett? Where's your Mercedes?"

"I'm not a banker. I'm a financial adviser in a bank. Along with a dozen other economists," he derisively tacked on.

"I still say you don't look the part," she maintained, unwrapping their pastries.

"It's the clothes," he told her. "You wouldn't recognize me in a suit."

Handing him a plastic fork, she mocked, "You mean you don't wear jeans and red shirts to work?"

"Hardly. But here I can indulge myself." His eye contact was volatile.

"You're the first indulgent economist I've met."

"You lucky girl, you!" He grinned.

Out of the blue Lisel found herself thinking: *I like him. I like him a lot. And I want to know more about him.* Aloud she invited, "Tell me about yourself."

"You already know practically everything there is to know. Your questioning yesterday was most comprehensive."

"You asked me just as many questions." She handed him his slice of *Sachertorte*. "More, in fact. Aren't you going to eat your cake?"—this as he studied her instead of his dessert.

"Of course I am." He sampled it and made *mmmm* sounds of approval. "How's yours?"

"Delicious." Lisel took another bite of her torte, the layered icing running over the curve of her upper lip. Her

42

tongue darted out to collect the excess, a procedure that Cas watched carefully.

"Does your family live in Chicago?" she asked.

"Yes. How about yours?"

"My uncle and his family live in Chicago."

"What about your parents?"

"They're in Atlanta right now. My dad works for an insurance company, and he gets transferred all around the country. I went to high school in four different states, but at least I got to complete a year in each one."

"Didn't you find it hard moving around so much?"

Lisel took another bite of her cake before replying, "It's all a matter of what you're accustomed to, I suppose. I have two sisters—one a year older, one a year younger—and we've always been pretty close. That helped. I also make friends easily. I guess I tend to make quick decisions about people, probably because I usually didn't have the time for a gradual acquaintanceship."

Which was why she'd been a ripe plum for Rick, Lisel silently reflected. Love at first sight had seemed perfectly natural to her. What did it matter if he had a few faults? No one was perfect. But Rick had expected her to be perfect and had complained bitterly because she wasn't. Drip by drip, like Chinese water torture, Rick's criticism had started a demoralizing erosion of self-confidence that Lisel was still in the process of repairing.

"A schilling for your thoughts," Cas softly offered.

"They're not worth it," she dismissed, angry with herself for thinking of Rick at all.

"If you want to talk, I've been told I'm a good listener."

"I've already gone on too much about myself. Let's talk about something else."

He quirked an eyebrow at her. "The weather?"

"It is a spectacular day. We had a lot of rain this summer, but the autumn so far has made up for it."

"At home we'd call this Indian summer."

Lisel made a sound of agreement, half-muffled by her chocolate cake. "Some people say that autumn is the gold at the end of the Alps' seasonal rainbow."

Their conversation became desultory as they soaked up the scenic serenity of their surroundings.

They made it back to Zell am See just as twilight was approaching. "Let's go down to the lake," she suggested. "Turn right at the next intersection."

"You want to go back to the scene of the crime?" Cas incredulously demanded, obeying her directions nonetheless.

"The alpenglow from there is fantastic."

"Alpenglow?"

"You'll see," she promised before pointing out, "there's a parking space over there."

Cas squeezed the Kadett into the cramped space.

"Come on!" She took his hand in hers to hurry him along a walking path that dead-ended at the lake.

Once there Cas saw what Lisel was talking about. The upper portions of the mountain peaks backing the lake were bathed in a flood of rose-colored light. As they watched in silent wonder, the alpenglow imperceptibly deepened to a lavender-crimson radiance. The light fell in splashes, igniting the snow-capped peaks with a layer of transparent red and thereby giving them the appearance of pyramids of fire. As the sun's rays weakened so did the intensity of the natural phenomenon until it disappeared altogether.

"Did you like it?" Lisel whispered, still awed by the chromatic magic.

"I like everything I've seen since coming to the Alps."

His inflection made Lisel turn her head to ask, "Everything?"

He nodded.

44

"Even that lethal fishhook?" she teased.

He flashed her a smile. "It did bring us closer together."

Lisel shivered at the recollection, her body remembering the passage of his hands.

"You're cold." He wrapped a protective arm around her shoulder and headed her back to the car.

Darkness fell quickly in the mountains, and it shielded Lisel's expression. In the close confines of the car she was overwhelmingly aware of every move Cas made. Each time he shifted gears her awareness grew. And since the car had a manual transmission, that meant a number of gearshifts! Consequently her emotions were running high by the time they returned to the Pension Traube.

After pulling into the cobblestone drive, Cas parked the car and cut the engine. "I think we may be in trouble here," he quietly announced.

"Trouble?" she stupidly echoed. "Is something wrong with the car?"

"Not with the car, no. With me."

"What is it?" Her concern was evident.

"The trouble is that I'm getting hooked. Hooked on you."

CHAPTER THREE

Now what are you going to do? Lisel silently panicked. *Jeopardize this relationship by backing off or risk a chance of history repeating itself?* Stalling the inevitable, Lisel asked, "What makes you think you're getting hooked?"

"This." His explanation took the form of actions rather than words. Wide masculine hands bracketed her face, the long fingers curving around the back of her neck to propel her forward. With unerring accuracy he homed in on her mouth, his tongue tracing the contours of her upper lip before lightly skimming the corners.

Lisel's lips gradually parted, sharing in the moment of discovery. For that's what his kiss held—lingering discovery. It was there in the intimate blending of advance and retreat. His lips played on hers until she was a more than willing participant.

Her hands, previously clenched in nervous fists, relaxed and joined in the exploration. Sliding up the hard resilience of his chest, they duly registered the increased rate of his heartbeat before continuing their restless searching. She felt the powerful flexing of his shoulders as he gathered her into him. Her hands came to rest at the base of his neck, her fingers hesitantly combing the dark hair brushing his collar.

Cas groaned softly, the sound entering her mouth and issuing a soothing caress for her tongue. His kiss took on a new slant, deepening and intensifying the contact between them. Lisel came alive in his arms, a warm, responsive woman who ended up hitting her knee on the gearshift!

"Ouch!" Her hands abandoned him and concentrated on soothing her bruised leg.

"I would've sworn I'd matured beyond making out in the front seat of a car," Cas murmured in a self-derisive tone. "But you have an overwhelming effect on me!"

Determinedly rubbing her leg, Lisel made no comment.

"I'm sorry about your knee," he commiserated, adding his ministrations to hers and intensifying her quandary.

What had she been thinking of? She couldn't afford to get involved with Cas; he was only passing through. Hadn't she learned a damn thing from her relationship with Rick? Hadn't she promised herself that she wouldn't make the same mistake twice?

"Cas, I can't—"

He pressed his fingers to her lips, those lips that he'd kissed so passionately only moments before. "I know. You've already told me. You don't want to get involved."

She nodded.

"That's why I told you we were in trouble. Because, honey, I'm already involved."

Lisel knew she should have been thinking about what to say next, but instead she found herself dwelling on the way he'd called her honey. She'd never been one for casual endearments, but this was the exception. Perhaps it was the expressive inflection of his voice; perhaps it was the lack of anything casual in his delivery. All she knew was that she liked it, that she liked him.

Her expression was troubled, her voice even more so as she murmured, "Oh, Cas." She slowly shook her head as if denying the force of her inner thoughts. What should she do? What should she say? She didn't want to jeopardize the promising passion they'd just shared, yet she wasn't prepared to go beyond that point.

Marshaling her emotions, she came to a decision. "Can't we just take things slowly? One day at a time?"

"All right," he eventually allowed. "One day at a time." Adding a smile, he asked, "How about tomorrow? What shall we do?"

"I thought perhaps we could go up to Moserboden."

"What's that?"

"It's an excursion up to a dam in the mountains. There are supposed to be some exceptional views from up there."

"Supposed to be," he immediately noted. "Haven't you been there before?"

Lisel shook her head. "I've only heard about it."

"Then Moserboden it is." He dropped a swift kiss on her lips. "I'm not going to promise that I won't kiss you."

"I guess I can't promise that I won't kiss you back either. But . . ."

"I know." They said the words simultaneously: "I don't want to get involved!"

They shared a smile in the darkness.

"We'd better go inside." Was that breathless voice hers? Taking charge of herself, Lisel calmly continued. "Maria wants to meet you."

"Wants to check me out, *hmm*?"

Lisel opened her car door. "You could say that."

Cas unfolded his legs from behind the steering wheel and got out of the car, then locked his door. "Then I guess that means I shouldn't tell her about rescuing you from

48

the lecherous clutches of a deadly fishhook?" he mused over the Opel Kadett's roof.

"Absolutely not!" She slammed the passenger door with more force than necessary.

Cas managed to inject a hilarious amount of expression into his simple "Oh."

Since Maria was almost as reluctant to use her English as Siggy was, Lisel was kept busy interpreting. When Maria's mother, a spry woman in her seventies, joined them the going really got tough. Oomah, as she was called, had a reputation for plain speaking. Lisel could only thank her lucky stars that Oomah was doing her plain speaking in German rather than in English.

"You've picked a nice young man here" was Oomah's first observation.

In German Lisel chastised her. "I didn't pick him."

Oomah was undaunted. "Nice, but his hips are too skinny."

"What did she say?" Cas asked Lisel.

"She hopes you're having a nice time here in Austria," Lisel fabricated.

"Tell her I'm having a wonderful time in Austria." Cas corrected her.

Lisel translated Cas's pleasantries and added, "He's not too skinny."

"I think a man should have plenty of meat on him," Oomah maintained.

"You want him as wide as a barn," Lisel accused.

Oomah shouted with laughter. "I don't want him, girl. I'm too old for him. But I'd say you're just about right. If you don't mind them skinny."

Lisel launched into a heated defense of his physique.

Cas had been viewing the exchange with some confusion. What could be so complicated about saying he was having a wonderful time in Austria? Consciously trying to

49

pick up a word or two of their dialogue, he was thrown by the dialect. But one word Lisel spoke he did recognize. "Sexy?" Cas threw her a quizzical look. "Am I missing something here?"

"I agree with Lisel," Maria inserted in German. "He is a very good-looking man."

Lisel shook her head despairingly. "If he understood what you two have been saying . . ."

"He would be looking more pleased than confused," Oomah incorrigibly stated.

"Oomah . . ." Lisel warned.

The spunky grandmother promised, *"Ich werde den Daumen halten."*

"Damen?" Cas misunderstood. "Doesn't that mean 'women'? It sounds like I am missing something here!"

"Damen does mean 'women,' but Oomah said *Daumen,* which means 'thumb.' "

"Is something wrong with her thumb?"

"No. It's part of a colloquial phrase. Like keeping your fingers crossed; only here it's called holding your thumbs."

Oomah demonstrated by shaking her fist.

"Who's she wishing luck to and why?"

"Umm . . ." Lisel managed some quick thinking. "She's wishing *me* luck." That was true.

"Why?" Cas asked.

"Why?" The best excuse she could come up with was "Because I've got to go cover the flower boxes on the balcony. It's going to get cold tonight."

"I'll help you." He raised a hand, precluding her argument. "And don't give me any hassle about guests' not helping."

"I wasn't going to," she denied. "I was merely going to thank you."

His lips slanted in the lopsided smile she was coming to know so well. "I'll collect my thanks in private later on."

Lisel was grateful to escape to the darkness of the balcony. Plastic sheets were neatly folded in one corner, ready to be spread over the array of chromatic flowers that any self-respecting Alpine balcony displays.

In her hurry to get outside, she'd omitted stopping for a jacket. The nippy night air helped clear her thoughts and was the primary reason for the hurried briskness of her movements.

"You're going to squash your petunias." Cas spoke in a dry voice.

The warning may have been unassuming, but the direction of his gaze was not!

When they were finished, Cas showed no eagerness to return to the warmth inside. "It's a beautiful night," he softly stated. "Just look at those stars. They're so close you could almost reach up and touch them."

"We came out here to work," Lisel reminded him. "Not stargaze."

"Look, there's Orion's belt."

"Where?"

Cas held her shoulders and aimed her in the proper direction.

After spotting the constellation he was referring to, her eyes roved to the right. At first she thought she was seeing things, but the star she was looking at was definitely moving!

"Cas!" In her excitement she grabbed his arm, shaking it for good measure.

"I had no idea you'd get so excited about Orion's belt," he mockingly murmured.

"It's moving!"

"What is?"

"That star up there."

51

"Are we about to have a close encounter?" he seductively suggested.

"I'm serious."

She missed his rueful expression as he said, "So was I."

"Cas, I'm not kidding. That star is moving!"

"Which one?"

"The second one over from the pink one at the end of Orion's belt."

Surprisingly enough Cas was able to follow her astronomical directions without any difficulty. "You're right! It is moving."

"What do you think it is?"

"Probably that new communications satellite the space shuttle just put up."

"Maybe it's one of those Russian spying satellites."

"In that case, let's give them something to spy on." With a swoop of his dark head he captured her startled mouth.

Hours later, in the privacy of her own room, Lisel could still feel the breathtaking imprint of his lips. Those memories colored her dreams with sensual shadings that left her bemused and smiling the next morning.

As she'd suggested yesterday, they headed for the Moserboden. The drive took them to the Kaprunertal, *Tal* being German for "valley." The road rose between steep mountainsides and dead-ended in a parking lot camouflaged by a stand of pine trees. They followed the parking attendant's directions for leaving the car in the already crowded lot.

"Here, give me your hand," Cas instructed once they had left the car. "I don't want anyone running over my tour guide."

"How considerate of you. Any more comments like that, and I'll leave you here!" Her mocking warning was accompanied by a sideways glance from her sparkling eyes.

"You wouldn't."

"Wouldn't I?"

"You're a cruel, cruel woman!"

"I know!" Lisel laughingly agreed, adding, "And don't you forget it."

"Why are you reaching for your wallet again?" he demanded. "When you come with me, it's my treat. I thought I'd already made that clear." Seeing that she was about to argue, he suggested, "Why don't you go to that kiosk over there and buy yourself some chocolate?"

Lisel relented but added the warning "You're not always going to be able to sidetrack me with chocolate."

"Honey, there will be times when I'll have no intention of sidetracking you."

How did his eyes manage to seduce her in the midst of a crowded parking lot? Let him loose on a romantic setting with candlelight, and she'd be in big trouble! But oh, what delicious trouble!

"Feeling the urge?" Cas softly questioned.

"Yes, I am," she softly replied, waiting a beat before adding, "for chocolate."

The triumphant grin was still on Lisel's face when she returned from the kiosk, chocolate bars in hand. "All set?" she asked Cas.

He nodded. "I've got both our tickets. The next group is leaving in five minutes."

"Will we be going by bus?"

"I couldn't get a clear answer on that one. My interpreter was satisfying her chocolate habit. All I know is that the tour starts by that door over there." He pointed to a pair of solid steel doors that appeared to lead directly into the base of a mountain.

53

"I'm beginning to have doubts about this," Lisel muttered, almost under her breath but not quite.

"What could go wrong?"

"Knock on wood when you say that."

Cas reached over and lightly tapped the paper wrapper of one of her chocolate bars.

"What are you doing?"

"You told me to knock on wood. This paper is the nearest wood by-product at hand."

She pointed toward the surrounding pine forest. "What about all these trees?"

"Too far away," he said dismissingly. "Besides, people would think I was nuts if I went around knocking on trees."

"They'd probably be right," Lisel quipped.

"Any more cracks like that, and I'll confiscate your chocolate bar."

"Saved by the doors." Lisel sighed in exaggerated relief as the double doors were pushed open from the inside. She and Cas followed the others who'd gathered near the opening and walked through the portal.

Looking at the seemingly endless expanse of tunnel before them, Lisel declared, "Now I *know* I'm having second thoughts!"

"Don't have claustrophobia, do you?" Cas questioned.

"I haven't up until now, but I'm making no guarantees. How about you?"

"No problem." He grabbed her hand. "Let's get moving before we're left behind."

"Wait a second. Let me find out where we're going first." She stopped a hiker whose traditional outfit included red-checked shirt, green corduroy knickers with matching knee socks, and hiking boots. After a rapid exchange of German she sighed and thanked him. "*Vielen Dank.*"

54

"Now what's wrong?" Cas asked.

"He said there's a ten-minute walk to the bus."

"That's not so terrible."

"You don't understand. To a serious hiker, a ten-minute walk could take the rest of us anywhere up to half an hour!"

Lisel's prediction was correct. Thirty minutes later they were still trudging down the tunnel. Every so often they'd pass under long sections of overhead pipes where the roar of rushing water made conversation impossible.

"The dam is used as a hydroelectric power station," Lisel explained. "A great deal of Austria's energy is water-powered."

"Sounds better than foot-powered energy. If I were two inches taller, I'd be in trouble," Cas noted, ducking under an overhanging slab of rough rock.

"Wait! I see something ahead!"

"It's probably a mirage. You've been in this tunnel so long you're starting to hallucinate!"

It wasn't a mirage, but it wasn't the hoped-for end of the line either. Instead it looked like some sort of underground substation.

Cas looked at the people milling around the steep set of metal steps. "What's everyone waiting for?"

"I have a feeling we're going to find out." Lisel had barely completed the sentence before a vehicle that looked like a cross between an elevator and a train descended from above and came to a halt. The top lifted, the sides lowered, and people got out.

"You've got to be kidding!" Cas exclaimed. "We're supposed to ride in that?"

"Don't look a gift horse in the mouth," she chided. "Would you rather walk all the way back?"

"No." He assisted her into the two-seat-wide vehicle. Joining her, he said, "You know this may have some

55

redeeming features after all. It's kind of cozy in here." His knee brushed against hers as the sides and the roof closed around them.

"Ouch!" he exclaimed a second later as her fingers dug into his knee. Her touch wasn't a brushoff but rather an expression of anxiety. "Hey, not scared, are you?" he murmured into her ear, wrapping an arm around her shoulder.

"I've never been overly fond of the dark," she admitted as the train began its forty-five-degree-angle ascent. The compartment had no interior lights, and the passageway they were traversing had only single dim light bulbs at long intervals.

"I don't know." His voice was ricocheted against her earlobe, clearly audible even over the train's rumbling. "The darkness has certain advantages."

Exhilaration surged through her veins. "Oh, like what?"

"Like this." Cas lowered his head to taste the warm and willing readiness of her lips.

Like this . . . her mind repeated his last words. Lisel didn't just like this; she loved it. She was fast getting hooked on his kisses, on his caresses. And that wasn't wise. But for the moment she didn't want to be wise. She wanted to kiss him.

Their arrival at the upper level became an intrusion, cutting short their embrace. They climbed out of their "gift horse" and progressed down another tunnel, a shorter one this time.

"I see daylight!" Cas gasped in exaggerated relief. Moments later they stepped out into the brilliant sunshine.

Pausing to allow their eyes to adjust to the change in light, they were addressed in English by an Austrian official. "The bus is that way."

56

"See," Cas said mockingly. "I told you there was a bus at the end of this tunnel."

They walked past the base of a huge dam several stories high and gratefully climbed aboard the waiting bus.

"Where do you suppose the road is?" Cas asked as he dropped down into the seat behind the driver.

"You're looking at it," Lisel answered, sitting next to him.

"That's not wide enough for a bus," he dismissed. "In fact, it's not even wide enough to be called a road. It must be a walking path."

"Want to bet?" Familiar with the outrageous narrowness of some Alpine roads, she challenged him.

"Sure. I'll bet you a *Sachertorte* that that path isn't the road."

"It's a bet!" A handshake sealed the deal.

The bus driver closed the door, and they were off, up the walking path that was indeed a road!

Cas's face paled, and his gulp was almost audible.

"Would you rather close your eyes?" she commiserated.

"How can you be afraid of the dark and be unfazed by this?" he muttered in confusion.

"The driver knows what he's doing," she assured him as they swung around a hairpin turn.

Cas, who was sure the front wheels had teetered over the edge, now looked decidedly green around the gills.

"Look, that's where we're going." Lisel pointed, hoping to distract him.

Before Cas got a chance to look, they'd entered another tunnel.

"Feel better now?" she asked.

"I'll feel better once we're up there."

And he did. It was hard not to with the breathtaking beauty of the surrounding scenery.

"These mountains surrounding the reservoir are part of the Hohe Tauern group."

A distant memory came to mind. "*Hohe* meaning 'high' in German?"

"Very good," she congratulated. "We'll have you talking like a native yet."

"I doubt that," he dryly denied.

"It's beautiful up here, isn't it?"

Cas agreed. The icy peaks of the Hohe Tauern mountain range provided some unforgettable vistas.

They strolled along the pathway that went across the top of the upper dam, Lisel munching on her chocolate bar while Cas took pictures.

Stopping in front of a sign, Lisel translated it for him. "That reservoir down there is called Wasserfallboden. *Wasserfall* means 'waterfall.' "

"Do you believe the color of that water?" He took a photograph.

"Makes a nice backdrop for those mountains in the distance, *hmm*?"

"Are those glaciers up there?" Cas asked.

"Sure are. There are a number of glaciers in this area. In fact, there's a large glacier up on the top of the Kitzsteinhorn where you can ski yearlong."

"Do you have to walk there?"

Lisel laughed at his pained expression. "No. There's a cable car that goes up."

"Then that's where we'll go tomorrow," he decided.

"But the Kitzsteinhorn is the mountain next door. The view is pretty much the same as this."

"Who's talking about the view? I'm talking about skiing."

"Skiing!"

"You don't ski?" Cas made it sound like a cardinal sin.

"Afraid not." Lisel shrugged.

58

"Why not?"

"I've never learned how."

"No problem. I'll teach you."

Lisel reminded him of his words the next morning when they stood on the gentle slope at the base of the glacier. Both their equipment and skiwear had been rented from a shop at the cable car station. Cas had already spent the past half hour on lesson number one—teaching her how to fall without hurting herself.

"I told you I wasn't very good at this," Lisel huffed, trying to get up after what must have been her fiftieth fall.

Cas lent her a helping hand. "You're doing fine." While she tried to regain her balance, Lisel's flailing elbow accidentally hit his ribs. *"Ooph."* The air whooshed out of his lungs.

"Are you okay?"

"I'm fine." He ruefully rubbed his chest.

"You're sure I didn't hurt you?"

"Not permanently anyway."

"I'm sorry. Maybe we'd better stop."

"No way. Come on, I was only kidding. Don't you want to experience the thrill of victory?"

"I'm afraid it will more likely be the agony of defeat. Are you sure I'm not going to break an arm or a leg doing this?"

"I'm sure."

"You promise?"

"Not only do I promise, but I'll put it in writing." He reached down and wrote something in the snow.

Lisel watched him, admiring his rented form-fitting black ski suit. This high up, over ten thousand feet, the sun was a potent heat source, so Cas hadn't bothered with a jacket, using a thick red ski sweater instead. The dramatic combination of red and black suited him. Her eyes ran

59

over his well-proportioned body—broad shoulders, trim waist, narrow hips, lean legs.

"There." He turned to face her, a wave of dark hair falling over his forehead. "Read it."

"You're in the way."

"Then I'll move." He did so with the ease of an expert skier.

Lisel laughed at the message he'd written in the snow. "LESSON 2—NO BROKEN BONES!"

Hearing the swoosh of approaching skis, she looked over her shoulder and caught sight of Cas approaching her from behind. Before she could voice a protest, he'd impelled her forward, his skis bracketing hers. His arms surrounded her and tugged her back into the cradle of his masculinity.

"How do you like skiing so far?" he wickedly questioned.

"I like it!" Lisel proclaimed.

"Bend your knees," he instructed.

"We're heading toward the barriers," she warned, indicating the snow-covered bales of hay cordoning off the safe skiing areas. "Cas!"

"It's all right. We're going to turn."

"We are?"

"We are." He guided her through a smooth turn and brought them both to a halt a few yards later. "See? It's not so hard."

"No, it wasn't."

"Ready for lesson number three?"

She nodded.

"This time you'll be skiing under your own steam."

"I don't know about that." Lisel dubiously tugged on her braid.

The section Cas had chosen to practice on was fairly

level, so it wasn't difficult to get back to their starting positions once more.

"I'll be right behind you," Cas promised her.

Going at a snail's pace, Lisel didn't find it as frightening as she'd expected. That lasted until Cas said, "Turn right."

"Left foot out, right?"

"Right. Use your pole," he reminded her.

Concentrating on her skis, Lisel had forgotten all about her poles. Which pole—left, right? She got confused.

"No, no! Turn right! The right's this way." He pointed with his ski pole.

Lisel executed a right turn that had more luck than technique.

Cas kept up his running commentary from directly behind her. "Okay, that was fine. Now turn left."

"I'm not good at turning left."

"Sure you are. Turn."

"Cas." Her voice reflected uncertainty.

"Left!"

"I can't!"

"Then turn right."

"I can't do that either," she wailed.

"Stop!"

That she did do, by falling down. Thanks to his earlier training, she didn't hurt anything other than her dignity.

"I told you I wasn't very good at turning left," she crossly complained. "Why did you have to ski me into the dirty snow?" She took a small handful of the gray slush and tossed it at him.

Cas retaliated by grabbing a handful of snow and throwing it right back, hitting the middle of her back. "Lesson number four: Never throw snow at your ski instructor."

"Oh, no?"

"No." He undid the bindings on his skis and joined her on the snow. "Kisses, on the other hand, are warmly appreciated."

His lips brushed across hers before he drew back to stare down at the glowing vitality of her face.

"You've got the strangest eyes," he murmured.

"Strange?" She bristled.

"Mmmm." Undaunted, he ran a finger across her lashes. "I can't tell if they're blue or green." He trailed a string of whispered kisses from her eyelid to her earlobe. "Where did you ever get such eyes?"

Lisel's arms reached up to curve around his neck, her fingers ruffling the dense thickness of his hair. "Genetic good fortune," she whispered against his jaw.

It was a simple matter to turn the near contact into something more. What began as a ghost of a kiss deepened into a form of exquisite seduction as their lips meshed in perfect accord. Tongues reveled in tastes and textures until reason was replaced by a rush of incandescent sensations, blinding them to the incongruity of their surroundings.

Pulled into a close embrace, Lisel arched her hips toward him. His seeking fingers sought and found the curve of her breast, but the bulk of her outer clothing formed an obstinate barrier. Her skis presented a further complication. This time it was Cas's turn to end their embrace with a smothered "ouch!" as her ski tip inadvertently hit his shin.

"Was this lesson number five?" she impudently questioned as he reluctantly released her.

"I think you're ready to progress to the advanced course," he rasped. "But in more suitable surroundings and when you're more suitably dressed. Or undressed!"

Her lack of outrage at his suggestion told her more forcefully than words how close she was to getting hooked. Each time Cas touched her, it got worse—because it felt better! Lisel had never experienced the simultaneous sensations of thrill and comfort as she did with him. Their physical recognition had been immediate, apparent from that first day when she'd given him a room. Fighting the attraction hadn't diminished it one bit. Even more dangerous was the fact that she no longer felt like fighting.

CHAPTER FOUR

Cas's stay at the Pension Traube stretched from three days to five to seven. During that time Lisel placed a moratorium on worry and concentrated on enjoying their developing relationship.

Observing the change in Lisel and correctly attributing it to Cas, Maria worried about Lisel's welfare. "How serious are things between you and Cas?" she asked Lisel on one of the rare occasions when they were alone together. As was their custom, their discussion took place in German.

Lisel feigned ignorance. "I don't understand."

"Don't give me that look. You understand German perfectly."

Lisel used the statement as an excuse to change the subject. "Have I thanked you and Siggy for having me spend the summer with you? It was a heaven-sent opportunity to improve my accent."

"Your accent is fine." Maria complimented her. "In fact, you speak like a native."

Lisel shook her head with a laugh. "There are still times

64

when you and Siggy get into that dialect of yours and I can't follow a thing."

"Ah, those are very private conversations!" Maria giggled.

"Oh? Like that, is it?"

"You're trying to change the subject," Maria scolded.

Lisel nodded and ruefully noted, "Apparently it didn't work."

"No. I am worried about you."

"Me? Why?"

"Because of Cas. How involved are you?"

"Pretty involved," Lisel admitted, thinking of the scene in the car last night. What had started as a simple kiss had ended as a passionate interval.

"Are you taking . . . precautions?" Maria asked delicately.

"We're not that involved!" Lisel protested with shock that was half-teasing, half-serious.

"Not yet perhaps. But I've seen you two together."

Oh, God, had Maria seen them in the car together?

"There are sparks between you even when you are across the room."

Lisel heaved a sigh of relief. They hadn't been seen. "Maria, you don't have to worry. I'm a big girl."

"That's precisely why I am worried!"

"Well, there's no need to be. I've been on the pill for several years now." Since before she'd met Rick, as a matter of fact. Her gynecologist had prescribed it for medical reasons.

Maria persisted in her questioning. "Has Cas said when he will be leaving?"

Lisel sighed reluctantly. "He can stay only three more days; then he has to catch his flight back to the States."

"What about you? Will you be leaving early to fly back with him?"

"We haven't really discussed it yet. Would you and Siggy mind if I did leave with him?"

"Not at all."

"Thanks a lot." She made a pretense of feeling hurt. "That eager to get rid of me, huh?"

"I did not mean that, and you know it. You are lucky to have the date of your return flight somewhat flexible. Johann said there would be no problem getting you a seat."

"How nice to have cousins in all the right places." Lisel grinned. "Siggy here, Johann working for the airline, and Hans in Chicago."

"It was quite a coincidence, you and Cas both living in Chicago. So romantic."

I hope so, Lisel thought in anticipation. She was too much in love to recite all the reasons she shouldn't be. The strange thing was that she couldn't pinpoint the exact moment when the knowledge of her love for Cas had come to her. It hadn't been at first sight, as with Rick. Oh, there had been physical attraction between her and Cas right from the start, but not love. This feeling was something else, something special. It was also something Lisel hadn't decided what to do about yet.

The next morning brought her no closer to a decision, despite a restless night spent worrying about it. Now there were only two days left before Cas's return to Chicago. As for her own return to Chicago, well, that was one of the things she had to talk about with Cas.

However, it wasn't something she could just casually bring up over the breakfast table, so instead she asked, "What should we do today?"

"You already know what I'd like to do," he drawled, adding a hungry look that warmed her soul.

Lisel did indeed know what he'd like to do, and so would she! But she could hardly do anything here right

66

under her family's watchful eyes. And she wasn't prepared to say, "I want to make love to you; let's go somewhere where we can be alone."

"What would you like to do today?" Cas asked, sensing her wavering but knowing she wouldn't appreciate his pushing his advantage.

"I don't know," she admitted through a sigh. "You haven't gone up the Grossglockner Road yet."

"Then let's do that today. It isn't too late, is it?"

Lisel had to smile at the ambiguity of his question. In many ways it was too late, too late to prevent herself from falling for him. But as far as the Grossglockner was concerned, the trip took about four hours, including stops for sight-seeing. That should leave plenty of time to get back before it got dark.

"No, it's not too late. Let me clear the table, and then we'll go."

She still wasn't used to the way Cas calmly pitched in as if it were the most natural thing in the world. Siggy, for all his devotion to his wife, wouldn't have been caught dead doing "women's work." And Rick was an expert excuse manufacturer.

Throughout the short time she'd known him Cas had constantly been surprising her—pleasantly surprising her. Lisel found herself studying his back, staring at the lumberjack shirt he wore as if its black and red checks held the answer to all her questions.

"Something wrong?" Cas asked, becoming aware of her intense scrutiny.

"No, nothing's wrong," she assured him, coming to terms with her internal indecisiveness. "Everything's right. Let's go."

Since the Grossglockner Road actually passed right in front of the Pension Traube, they had no problem finding it. Before reaching the toll booth, they passed a sign assuring them that the road ahead was open. "Are you sure you won't let me split the toll with you?" Lisel offered while Cas pulled the Kadett in line behind a roomy Mercedes.

"Positive. Just sit back and guide me."

"Guide you? Like this?" Her hand reached out to trail along his thigh. "I'm not sure you would be able to concentrate on your driving if I did that," she drawled in a seductive murmur before removing her hand.

Their arrival at the toll booth prevented Cas from responding. After paying the required toll, he handed Lisel the map and bumper sticker he'd been given, adding a deceptively bland "This road must have turnoffs." There was nothing bland, however, about the way his eyes ranged over her curves!

"To look at the scenery, yes."

"I wouldn't mind admiring your scenery," Cas outrageously suggested.

Lisel's heart caught in her throat, suspending her breathing and dissolving the courage that had led her to tempt him in the first place. Concentrating on the map he'd given her, she studiously noted, "There are twenty-six hairpin turns on this road."

"Don't worry about a thing." He shifted into first and then patted her denim-clad knee. "I'm very good at negotiating curves."

Teasing though his touch may have been, it still had the power to make her long for more. Hoping to distract him—and herself!—she continued her recitation about the road they were traversing. "During construction Roman relics were found, indicating that this same route was being used by traders and warriors over two thousand years ago."

"Fascinating!"

"I know," she said in agreement, being a history fan herself.

68

"No, I meant us."

"We're fascinating?"

"Don't you think so?"

"I'm not sure that 'fascinating' is the adjective I would use," she said doubtfully, thinking more along the lines of "sexy" or "combustible."

"What adjective would you use then?"

"'Unique'?" she suggested, refusing to voice her original choices.

"Unique." He said it as if testing the word for flavor. The shake of his head indicated his disfavor. "I prefer 'fascinating.' Or 'perfect.'"

"There speaks a modest economist."

He grinned a naughty grin. "Hey, I know a great limerick about modest economists!"

"I can imagine," she dryly retorted.

"Can you? I had no idea you knew any dirty limericks."

"Appearances are deceiving."

"Yours aren't." His gaze roved over her turquoise angora sweater, impudently resting on the provocative upthrust of her breasts. "They're beautiful!"

Lisel issued a protesting "Cas!" blessing the fact that she didn't blush.

"What did I say?" he innocently inquired.

"It wasn't what you said; it was where you were looking."

"I was just admiring the scenery."

"Try concentrating a little more on the mountain scenery and a little less on mine."

"I suppose that would be safer." He sighed, then made sure to tack on, "For the time being."

While they'd been exchanging quips, the sky had become more cloudy than sunny. "I hope it's not going to get socked in," Lisel murmured.

"The clouds seem to be moving quickly. That should help."

Lisel checked his observation. The clouds were indeed moving quickly. That meant the Foehn was blowing. She began having feelings of misgiving. Maybe she should have checked the weather report before they'd left. But she reminded herself that the Foehn could blow in good weather as well as bad.

"It's the Foooon," Cas heard her say.

"The Foooon?" he repeated in confusion. "Are you practicing an Inspector Clouseau impersonation?"

His question brought a laughing return of her good humor. "You're a Peter Sellers fan, too, huh? Fascinating!" Her use of his adjective was deliberate. "But I wasn't imitating our favorite French inspector's unusual accent. The Foehn is a wind that blows up from the south and causes a change in the weather."

"Change for the good or change for the bad?"

"That's the question."

"Tell me some more about the road. And before I forget, why did those signs back at the toll booth call this the GroBglockner Road?"

"You obviously didn't pay attention in your high school German class," she scolded.

"I was too busy trying to attract the attention of a little cheerleader two rows across from me."

"Oh?"

"No need to sound jealous." Cas tossed her a teasing grin. "She married the captain of the football team, and they now have five kids."

"Good for her. And to answer your question, that slightly strange capital *B* is actually the German equivalent of a double *s*. Ah, here's the first hairpin turn."

Cas handled the car like a pro, not overcompensating

for the steep angle and completing the turn without having to downshift.

"Where did you learn to handle mountain driving so well?" she asked.

"I'm adept at handling things."

"I have to agree with you, speaking from personal experience," she pertly added.

"Maybe we should stop and I'll give you another example."

"We wouldn't want to steam up the windows," she demurely stated.

"Wouldn't we? Speak for yourself."

"While we're on the subject, I never asked you where you learned how to ski."

He eyed her with reprimanding mockery. "That's not the subject we were on, and you know it."

"It's the subject we're on now," she resolutely maintained. "Where did you learn how to ski so well?"

"Not in Chicago, that's for sure," he retorted.

"I guessed that much for myself."

"Clever girl," he congratulated her. "I did two years of undergraduate work at the University of Denver and took a lot of excursions up into the Rockies. Did you want to stop at the next turnoff?"

"Yes, but to admire the view, not to steam up the windows."

"Spoilsport."

"Sticks and stones . . ." she taunted.

"It isn't my intention to break your bones. I've got a much more pleasant prospect in mind for your delectable body."

"I wouldn't touch that line with a ten-foot pole."

"How about a five-foot-eleven Pole?" he asked after parking the car in the scenic turnoff.

71

Lisel groaned and shoved her door open. "A pun like that deserves corporal punishment."

"Sorry. I couldn't resist."

"Since this was your first offense, I'll forgive you."

"What a generous guide I've got."

His words served to remind Lisel of her duty. "Then as your guide I should tell you that Austria is the most mountainous country in Europe."

"Not Switzerland?"

"No. The mountains cover three-fifths of Switzerland, but here the proportion is two-thirds."

"That surprises me."

"Then Austria's size should also surprise you. It's only as large as the state of Maine."

"Good things come in small packages."

"So they say." It was silly to be disgruntled, but Lisel was very much aware that she was no small package. If standing five feet eight inches in bare feet wasn't bad enough, she also had what she considered Junoesque proportions. Granted, her 36B figure didn't make her any Dolly Parton, but still . . .

"What are you frowning at?" Cas demanded.

"The weather," Lisel fibbed. Although now that she looked at it, the outlook didn't appear to be very good. "It looks like it's getting socked in."

"At least we got to see the mountains on the way up."

"I was hoping to show you the view of the Grossglockner itself. It's the tallest mountain in Austria, you know."

His mocking "No, I didn't know" made her ruefully apologize. "Sorry. Was I coming on too strong as a tour guide?"

"Honey, you can come on to me anytime you like."

Their flirtatious banter dispelled Lisel's worries about the weather as she concentrated her attention on Cas. But after they had returned to the car and continued their ascent, it was impossible to ignore the situation any longer. The higher they got, the worse the weather became.

First came the damp drizzle, which gradually turned into huge snowflakes in the higher, and therefore colder, elevations. By that time they were so far along the road that it was more expeditious to continue on than to turn around. The cars on the road became few and far between. That was a blessing because the visibility also became increasingly bad.

Cas's knuckles showed white as he gripped the Kadett's steering wheel, his eyes frowning in concentration. Lisel's figure reflected a similar tenseness. The situation was deteriorating rapidly. Snowflakes bumped into each other in their swift descent, forming a mantle of white clusters. At times the direction of the road was barely discernible through the folds of swirling snow. When one considered that a wrong turn could mean an eight-thousand-foot drop, it was easy to understand the worried silence in the car.

"Look on ahead and see if you can see anyone coming," Cas suggested as they neared another hairpin turn.

Since the road backtracked on itself, looking ahead actually meant looking out the back window. Lisel offered a silent prayer for rear-window defrosters and wipers before saying, "All clear!"

Cas swung the car around, keeping the speed as steady as he could. If he went too fast, they were likely to skid. If he went too slow, the tires could get mired down in the snow. They made it around the turn with only a minimal amount of sliding. The steep gradient of the road, twelve percent at times, was another dangerous factor. With slippery traction the car was apt to roll backward if the forward momentum wasn't just right.

The Opel Kadett valiantly pressed on while the slate-colored cloud layer shed an opaline light peculiar to snowstorms. Sound was muffled, strengthening the sense of solitude. The mountains had long since faded off into chalky blankness, like a painting that had been left half-finished.

Cas had his window rolled down a crack, trying to listen for the sound of approaching traffic. It was this early-warning system that alerted them to the sound of a snow-plow, which appeared seemingly out of nowhere and came within inches of their car as it uncaringly swept by. Lisel silently seconded Cas's muttered expletives, adding a few German ones for good measure.

Darkness had fallen by the time they descended the snowy heights only to be engulfed in misty fog at the lower altitudes. Continuing in this weather would be dangerous, especially after the nerve-racking drive they'd just completed. The decision to stop at the first available hotel was a mutual one. A short time later they gratefully welcomed the lights of a roadside inn.

That welcome, however, was not returned by the stern-faced clerk behind the registration desk.

"We'd like a room, please," Cas requested in English.

"Certainly, sir." The man impassively eyed their luggageless state. "One room or two?"

"That depends on how much they cost," Cas retorted, the economist in him coming to the fore.

The desk clerk's glance at Cas and Lisel's casual attire suggested that this establishment was beyond their meager means. "The only rooms we have left are higher-priced."

Cas held on to his patience with difficulty. "How high is high?"

The desk clerk pulled out a pamphlet listing room prices and proceeded to circle the deluxe column. "These are the only rooms available." A phone call then demanded his attention, leaving Cas and Lisel in relative privacy.

74

"So how high is high?" Cas repeated, this time directing his question to Lisel, who was studying the pamphlet.

"For two rooms it would work out to be about a hundred and a half," she quickly calculated.

"Schillings?"

"Dollars."

"That is high."

Lisel agreed. "Especially in light of the fact that I have only the equivalent of twenty dollars with me. I wasn't planning on getting marooned."

"Neither was I, but I do have a credit card."

"Did you want one room or two?" the desk clerk impatiently demanded of them, having completed his phone call.

"One," Lisel answered on both their behalfs. Her murmured "We can work out the details later" was for Cas's ears only.

Their room was on the second floor, facing what would normally no doubt have been a fantastic view. But now all that could be seen through the darkness was a blank wall of fog. Lisel drew the drapes shut.

As she turned to survey the rest of the room, her attention centered on the built-in double bed flanked by a pair of carved wooden wardrobes. Suddenly she began having second thoughts about the advisability of this arrangement. She and Cas would be sharing that bed tonight—sharing the bed and what else?

"Shall we go down for some dinner?" Cas courteously asked, seeing the sudden tensing of her shoulders.

"That sounds like a good idea," she answered, eager to leave the homey intimacy of the room and the even more disturbing intimacy of her own thoughts.

A good dinner complete with a glass of Rhine wine went a long way toward relaxing her tension. Cas went out of his way to set her at ease so that by the time they returned to their room, their customary rapport had them exchanging mocking quips. After placing a call to Fusch and assuring Siggy of her safety, Lisel was all set to call it a night.

"What are we going to use for sleepwear?" she asked with sensible practicality.

"For you, the very shirt off my back!" Cas peeled off the plaid shirt and handed it to her with a flourish. Since he wore a black turtleneck sweater under it, the shirt had actually served more as a jacket.

She accepted it, fingering the flannel material that still retained his body warmth. "What about you?"

"Don't ask personal questions," he reprimanded, adding one more instruction. "You just go use the bathroom first."

Thankfully the hotel provided a complimentary array of personal hygiene needs. There was toothpaste but no brush, so she used her index finger as a weapon against tooth decay. The discovery of a compact blow dryer provided her with the means to dry her bikini undies and bra after she'd washed them in the sink. Then she took the liberty of using the pine-scented soap and the package of bubble bath, unable to resist the temptation of a short soak in the huge ceramic tub.

After toweling herself dry, she donned her unusual nightgown. Cas's shirt only reached down to her mid-thigh, not a very modest length but better than nothing at all. Besides, her newly dried panties were back in place. Telling herself that a beach wrap would have been equally revealing, Lisel opened the bathroom door.

Hoping to ease the momentary tension, she strolled across the room, lightheartedly suggesting, "If I were Claudette Colbert and you were Clark Gable, we'd shove the beds apart and hang a blanket between them."

Cas lay sprawled across the foot of the bed, looking

completely at ease. "First off, these beds don't have blankets—only down comforters—and if you use that for anything other than keeping warm, you'll freeze. Secondly, I don't think we can move the beds apart; they're built in. Thirdly, and most important, I'm not Clark Gable, and you bear no resemblance to Claudette Colbert. Except maybe for your legs."

"My legs?" Lisel eyed that part of her anatomy as if she'd never seen them before.

"You're not the only one who's seen the movie *It Happened One Night.* Claudette has great legs—she stopped traffic with them if I recall correctly. But it's no contest." His visual appreciation was rich with masculine approval and was accompanied by an indrawn whistle. "Yours are sexier by a long shot! In fact, they're the first thing I noticed about you. I walked into the pension, and there you were, leaning over a credenza and displaying a generous amount of gorgeous tanned leg just for me."

Lisel hadn't been aware that the hem of her black uniform's skirt rose that considerably. "I was arranging flowers, not displaying myself for you."

"Don't ruin my fantasies," Cas ordered.

"I wouldn't dream of it," she teasingly acquiesced.

A sudden silence followed her words, marking a return of tense awareness. The intimacy of their surroundings and the temptation of their proximity all served to fuel the fires of desire.

"Have the lights out by the time I'm out of the bathroom." Abandoning his casual position on the bed, Cas issued the abrupt order and then stalked out of the room.

Lisel knew better than to object, and the lights were duly doused well before he returned. She felt the bed sag slightly as he got in under his individual twin-size comforter. She heard the rustle of the damask cover as he tugged on it impatiently. She smelled the same faint scent of pine that clung to her own skin. How had he looked, standing under the shower she'd heard him run? She imagined him without the constraint of clothing, and her blood grew warm. Was he wearing anything besides that whiff of pine?

Consumed with prowling needs, Lisel moved restlessly under her individual comforter. Simultaneously Cas breathed an exasperated sigh. The minutes passed, with more restless movement from Lisel and increasingly audible sighs from Cas. They lay, facing opposite directions, both unable to sleep. Turning in unison, they suddenly found themselves face-to-face with a scant few inches separating them.

"This wasn't a good idea," he growled, the minty freshness of his breath warm on her face.

"What wasn't?" she asked, even though she already knew.

"Sharing a bed." His voice was roughened by desire. "I'm trying to be a gentleman. But, honey, I'm fighting a losing battle."

"Then stop fighting," she softly suggested.

There was a perceptible pause before Cas huskily questioned, "Does that mean what I think it means?"

"I guess it does" was her purring agreement.

"In that case, come here." His arms reached out for her even as he spoke.

Their lips merged with undeniable hunger. The shivers chasing up Lisel's spine were rapidly followed by flares of warmth. The feverish symptoms were reflected in the avid ardor of her response as her white teeth evocatively nibbled at his lower lip.

Stroking the pearly gates of her mouth, his questing tongue soon gained admittance. Tasting and teasing, Cas kissed her with a daring intimacy that stole her breath. Only when their lungs demanded it did his mouth ease away to rain gossamer kisses across her face. The determined point of her chin, the curve of her cheekbones, the vulnerability of her temples—all these were adored as though each were precious to him.

The velvety concavity of her ear was the last recipient of his attention. His enticing tongue spearheaded the sensual assault, which culminated in his husky whisper. "Honey, I've fallen in love with you."

Already reeling from the impact of his tantalizing caresses, Lisel was dazed by his words. Her stammered "Cas . . ." was halted by his restraining finger pressed to her lips.

"*Shhhh.*" His raspy murmur assailed her senses, wrapping her in its warmth. "You don't have to say anything. Just let me show you."

"Oh, yes," she moaned. "Yes, Cas."

Threading his fingers through the silken waterfall of her hair, he tilted her head back and kissed the long line of her throat. His lips traversed the path of every throbbing pulse until the impassioned magic of his touch permeated her skin and coursed through her bloodstream. When the flannel shirt obstructed his further exploration, its buttons were undone with a deftness that reminded Lisel that it was his shirt she was wearing.

His knuckles brushed against the valley between her breasts as his lips nudged aside the open V of the shirt and kissed the satiny skin laid bare to him. The hollows of her throat were the first recipients of the tiny, reverent kisses. The base of her collarbone was next. By the time his caresses lowered to her shadowed cleavage, she felt the added pleasure of a swirling tongue arrowing in between the creamy fullness of her breasts.

The shirt was now completely unbuttoned, so his hands were free to part the partial covering gently and remove it altogether. There was a forthright sensuality in the way he held her, a loving certainty in the way his hand moved to cup her breasts. Their fullness had always been a source of self-conscious embarrassment to Lisel, who longed for the sleek smallness of a 32A.

As though tuned to her every thought, Cas sensed her discomfiture and guessed the reason for it. His assurance was husky as he feathered his thumb across a rose-tipped crest. "You're . . . perfect. . . ." Each pause was punctuated with a kiss to her trembling lips. "Lush . . . ripe . . . incredibly tempting!"

His mouth descended to lightly cajole each dusky peak, transforming them into taut nubs, which he then caught between his teeth. His warm tongue sent shock waves of pleasure fluttering through her as he sampled the taste of her. Deep in her abdomen, desire hit her like a blow.

The fingers of her left hand curled into the springy thickness of his hair, binding him closer while the more adventurous fingers of her right hand sought out the smooth curves of his spine. Practicing an intuitive knowledge, she lovingly surveyed each vertebra until he slid out of her reach.

Lisel was left momentarily bereft until she realized his intent. His mouth moved downward from the temptingly erect tips of her breasts to the lower slopes of her abdomen. Tunneling his fingers beneath the slender side panels of her bikini briefs, he soon had dispensed with them.

Stretching out her hands, Lisel brought him back up beside her. She reproduced his actions until he too was nude. Her fingers were then free to caress him at will—from his powerful shoulders to his lean hips. She felt the involuntary contraction of his muscles as her gliding caresses proclaimed her prodigious feminine power.

"God, honey!" His voice was a hoarsely disturbed whisper. "I can't wait any longer."

Eliminating what little space there'd been between

them, Cas molded her supple body to his taut nakedness. His knee nudged her legs apart, sensuously sliding up and down the inner curve of her thighs. Despite his earlier avowals of need, Cas leashed his own ardor in order to ignite hers. Displaying finesse as well as skill, his hand sought and received permission to woo her final threshold. His intimate touch stole the last remnants of her composure.

His mouth stifled Lisel's expressions of hunger with a kiss that was triumphantly passionate. Ruled by desire she boldly offered herself, her hands making impelling demands on his masculinity. She felt the shudder that racked his body and gloried in the realization that she could shatter his composure the way he'd shattered hers.

The time for waiting was done, annihilated by a meteoric burst of imperative need. With an intricate thrust, the agony of aching emptiness was transformed into the thrill of completion. Shimmering warmth ebbed and flowed as they both moved as one—the undulation of his hips matched by the arching of hers. Wave upon wave of recurrent undulations pulsated though her entire being, intensifying into a towering crescendo that apexed in the raw ecstasy of their mutual release.

CHAPTER FIVE

Vanquished by the afterglow of their lovemaking, Lisel lay with her face nestled in the hollow of Cas's throat. Her lips monitored his throbbing pulse as it slowed from the racing heat of passion to the steady cadence of satisfaction. The fingers of her right hand absently soothed the muscled planes of his chest, luxuriating in the firmness of his male flesh.

Cas pressed a soft kiss to the crown of her head, his hand drifting through the strands of her long hair as if fascinated with its silky texture.

Her voice heavy with drowsy intensity, Lisel finally got a chance to speak the words she'd meant to say earlier. "I love you."

His fingers stilled in her hair. "What?"

"You heard me." She pressed a tiny kiss against the bare skin of his shoulder. "I said I love you."

Cas crooked one finger under her chin, tipping her head back so that she looked up at him. "Are you sure?" he breathed.

82

"I wouldn't be with you like this if I weren't." The love she had for him was glowing in her eyes.

He entwined his fingers in her hair, the subtle pressure directing her into his kiss. Lisel reveled in the sensual curve of his mouth. Her tongue was tantalized by his warm taste as she showered him with kisses. The force of her ardor drove him back against the pillows. His hands were clasped behind her head, bracketing her between the muscular strength of his forearms and the sensuous slant of his kiss. Their embering passion soon sparked into a sultry flame.

By small degrees, Cas drew her closer until they fitted together with erotic precision. Shifting her leg in lambent hunger, she felt his resurging arousal. His body tightened in eager anticipation as her fingers grazed down the line of his rib cage. Her caresses were on the verge of becoming undeniably provocative when Cas suddenly slipped from her embrace and left the bed.

"Where are you going?" she demanded in thwarted astonishment.

He stood there, wearing a devilish smile and nothing else. "I'll be right back!"

Lisel barely had time to admire the perfection of his body before he strode toward the door. The reality of him was even more stimulating than her imaginings had been.

The hallway was deserted so no one saw the door to room 219 quickly open and close. The only hint of activity was the newly placed multilingual "PLEASE DO NOT DISTURB" sign that was swinging from the doorknob!

The sound of Cas's voice woke her the next morning. ". . . and I'd like a pot of hot coffee, please."

A pot of hot coffee? Was Cas giving her orders already? She peered at him through one half-opened eyelid, viewing the rippling muscles of his back as he hung up the phone.

Seeing her flickering lashes, he leaned over to kiss the curve of her shoulder. "Morning, sleepyhead."

She saw that he'd donned his jeans. "What time is it?"

"Almost ten." He nibbled his way along her shoulder. "That's why I called room service." His voice was muffled against her bare skin. "They stop serving in another five minutes."

"I see." She shivered as his nibbling reached her earlobe, then squealed as he took a playful bite. "Do you plan on assuaging some of your hunger on my tender anatomy until your food arrives?"

His face lit up with unholy amusement. "Now there's an idea."

Unfortunately a sharp knock on the door prevented the enactment of any prebreakfast feasting.

Cas lifted his head from the tempting curve of her throat. "Ah, room service."

"Where are you going?" she sat up to demand, unaware of the slipping comforter. "I don't have any clothes on."

"I know." His eyes ran over her, appreciating the impertinent tilt of her breasts. "And damn tempting you are, too. But, honey, a man does not live by lovemaking alone! I'm starving!"

She shot him a patrician look and regally announced, "I'll wait in the bathroom." Her attempt at queenly behavior, however, was soon ruined. Lisel ended up scampering past a chuckling Cas as he made threatening motions to let in the now impatient waiter.

A few minutes later Cas rapped on the bathroom door and called, "It's all right. You can come out now."

Lisel had used the intervening time to wrap one of the hotel's generous bath sheets around her. For once she found herself appreciating her proportions, for they certainly helped keep the towel in place!

"Close your eyes and open your mouth," Cas seductive-

84

ly instructed from just beyond the now open bathroom door.

Lisel obeyed, sensual anticipation bringing out goose bumps along the bare expanse of her arms. Her lips were parted, eager for his kiss. But instead they received a buttery portion of croissant.

"You're a tease, Cas Kalensky!" Her accusation was made through a mouthful of croissant.

His face wore a "who me?" expression as he cupped her face with his hand and said, "You've got a dab of cherry jam on your chin."

"I do?" she mumbled, then swallowed her unexpected treat.

"Allow me." His head dipped closer so that his tongue could flick across her skin.

"Thank you," she calmly stated once he had stepped away. "But now you've got jam smeared on your mouth. Allow me," she purred.

Lisel made the most of the opportunity, her tongue inflicting a lightning attack on his senses. Her cajoling had his lips hungrily claiming hers. That's when she stepped away with a satisfied grin and said, "I'm hungry. Let's eat!"

"Talk about me being a tease . . ."

Her reply was dripping with self-dramatization. "I'm a fast learner."

"You certainly are!" he ruefully agreed. He held out a chair for her with a fastidious courtesy that would've made even the most supercilious waiter green with envy.

"Thank you, kind sir."

Lisel would never forget that shared breakfast—the long, lingering looks, the tantalizing touches, the evocatively romantic words. Her buoyant mood lasted throughout the return trip to Fusch. Since the Grossglockner

Road had been closed as a result of the heavy snowfall, they had to use the Felbertauern tunnel route.

With the appropriate changeableness of mountain weather, the skies were now clearing. On the lower pine-covered slopes, spots of green pasture were already visible through the shrinking blanket of snow. The generous dollop of snow made the surrounding mountains seem even more impressive. Several of the highest peaks, including the Grossglockner, were still draped with snow clouds.

"You know, despite all the trouble it put us through yesterday, the snow really does look magical."

"The Alps are full of magic," Lisel dreamily acknowledged.

"That's for sure." In the process of shifting gears, his fingers reached out to trail up her denim-clad thigh. "And very sexy magic it is, too!"

"I wasn't talking about that kind of magic," she wryly stated. "I was belatedly trying to fulfill my duties as your guide."

Regretfully his fingers had to return to the steering wheel. "Then, by all means, continue."

"The Alps haven't always been a popular tourist haven. Until the eighteenth century these mountains were considered the dwelling place of evil spirits and dragons."

"Dragons, huh?" His mouth kicked up into a smile. "With bat wings and long, hairy tails?"

"Those are the ones. According to legend, these dragons would fly over the mountains and drop stones that had miraculous powers."

"Did they also drop snow?" he mockingly asked as they entered the tunnel.

But Lisel didn't hear his question. A simple thing, like his flicking on the car's headlights, had prompted a chain of memories. Memories of last night, when she'd kissed the supple strength of those wrists. *You've really got it bad*

86

if you think wrists are sexy, she told herself. But then she thought every inch of Cas was sexy!

Coming out of her reverie, she murmured, "Did you ask me something?"

"Never mind," he ruefully dismissed. "Thanks for telling me that bit of local superstition."

"Superstition?" she mocked. "I'll have you know that a fellow of the Royal Society of London actually published a catalogue of Alpine dragons."

"In that case, you're lucky to have a knight in shining armor accompanying you," he told her with a disarming grin.

Indeed, Lisel did feel lucky, and she mentally recited the reasons why. Because Cas had chosen the Pension Traube. Because she'd let him stay. Because Cas returned her love, and how! He was a passionate and tender lover, a stunning combination of conquering hero and wooing suitor.

With her thoughts following such a romantic trail it was inevitable that she'd jump to conclusions when Cas said, "You know, there's something I've been meaning to ask you."

A proposal? Of what? Living together? Marriage? Taking a deep breath, she prompted, "Go ahead."

"What's a *Wurzeln?*"

Lisel blinked in disbelief. "What?"

"A *Wurzeln?*" he patiently repeated. "I've been seeing these signs for them each time we get on this road back to Fusch."

So much for romance! she silently noted with resigned humor. "*Wurzeln* means 'roots.' The signs advertise workshops that sell carvings made from roots."

"Carvings from roots? This I've gotta see!" he said, deliberately exaggerating his enthusiasm.

The inside walls of the shop were covered with wood

carvings of gnarled and wizened faces. Each held an individual appeal decided in a large part by the direction of the carving's eyes. A downward gaze projected humility; upward, pious devotion. But Lisel's favorites were the ones with sidelong glances because they suggested a teasing mischievousness reminiscent of Cas. Apparently he thought so, too, because he bought the most audacious carving and presented it to Lisel.

"For you. Something to remember me by."

Lisel was frightened by the tenor of his words. They'd sounded suspiciously like a farewell. "Are you leaving?" she questioned.

"You know I am. Tomorrow." He looked around the small shop. "I realize this isn't the most auspicious place to ask, but is there any chance of your coming back with me?"

His question burst the dam of fear blocking her throat, releasing a flow of words. "There's a very good chance. And it wouldn't be any problem because my cousin Johann works for the German airlines. You're flying out of Munich, right? And connecting in Frankfurt?"

"Whoa!" Cas laughingly held up his hand. "I gather that you would be interested in returning with me?"

"You gather correctly," Lisel avowed, wishing they were alone so she could throw her arms around him.

Via that silent means of communication they shared, Cas divined her thoughts and linked his fingers through hers. "Later."

But later didn't arrive before their departure. Once they'd returned to the Pension Traube, their time was split between talking to Siggy and Maria and packing. Lisel lay alone in her own bed that night, remembering the passion shared the night before.

Their noon flight out of Munich necessitated an early-morning departure from Fusch. Lisel was awake well before her alarm went off at six. Gathering up the last of her possessions, she paused to gaze out her window. No matter how many times she saw it, she never failed to be moved by two of the mountain's most magical moments—sunrise and sunset. Night's dark shade lifted slowly, revealing the tender daffodil aurora that heralded the approach of a new day. Ribbons of frothy pink clouds added a new splash of color as the iridescent dawn broke over the jagged horizon.

Lisel would miss these mountains, miss them terribly. She'd had a wonderful summer here, culminating in her discovery of Cas. The damage Rick had done to her self-confidence had been repaired, thanks to the healing Alpine surroundings and the strength of Cas's love.

Maria's knock on her door ended Lisel's early-morning reflection. That plus the fact that she had only fifteen minutes to get dressed. Since she made it with thirty seconds to spare, she used that time to check her appearance in the mirror. For the purpose of traveling, she'd fastened her hair in its customary braid. The warm rust of her slacks and matching jacket complemented her coloring. And her makeup showed no hint of the haste with which it had been applied! "Good." She nodded approvingly at her reflection.

All too soon it was time to leave. Their departure was made amid tearful farewells and warm hugs from Siggy and Maria. Lisel surreptitiously wiped her damp eyes as Cas directed the Opel Kadett toward Munich. They used the route via Salzburg even though it was less direct, because the road was an autobahn.

They made good time, the only delay occurring at the border between Austria and Germany, and that was due only to the heavy morning traffic. After a bored official had checked their passports, they were waved on through as just another pair of American tourists. Now that they were in Germany, the autobahn became more like a race-course. Road signs warned of staying in the right lane, using the left lane only for passing. Lisel knew from experience that that was due to incredible speeds the passing cars maintained.

"I find it hard to believe there's no speed limit at all on this thing," Cas muttered when a maroon Mercedes passed them as if they were standing still. "I'm doing a hundred thirty kilometers an hour, so you can imagine what his speed was."

"Your speed's bad enough. You're doing about eighty miles per hour."

"That should get us to Munich right on schedule."

But they hadn't reckoned on the heavy traffic clogging the city's inner expressway ring, which made them late. Consequently, their check-in at Munich's airport was a hurried affair. Cas returned the car to the rental agency while Lisel took care of checking their luggage and obtaining seats. Johann hadn't let her down—her ticket was waiting for her at the ticket desk.

Cas joined her shortly thereafter, and they rushed through the airport's heavy security procedures before boarding their plane for Frankfurt. It was a short flight, a little under an hour—barely time to take off, serve drinks, and land again. There was also little time for conversation, and for that reason the loss of their customary rapport wasn't immediately discernible.

But once they were on board the full 747 to Chicago and well over the Atlantic, it was impossible to ignore the creeping sense of awkwardness any longer. Suddenly Cas was no longer looking at her when he spoke to her. And his voice reflected none of the special warmth she had come to count on.

Under the pretext of taking a nap, Lisel closed her eyes. Her mind was then free to play the "What if" game. What if Cas was regretting telling her he loved her? What if he wished she hadn't come with him? What if she'd made a mistake? What if this was just a holiday fling, not the real thing?

All Lisel knew was that the closer they got to Chicago, the quieter and more awkward things became between her and Cas. Their conversation was absolutely stilted as they picked at the airline's idea of dinner. Upon their landing at O'Hare International Airport their attention centered on the bureaucratic formalities of immigration and customs.

Only when they'd left the arrival hall did Cas say, "Do you have someone meeting you, or would you like to share my ride? I ordered a limo to meet me."

Confused by his increasing coolness and angered by his indifferent invitation, Lisel retorted, "No, I don't have anyone meeting me, but I can catch a cab."

"Don't be ridiculous. I'm going that way anyway. Come on." He grabbed one of her suitcases and strode out the door, heading toward a long black Lincoln Continental with a carriage emblem on the door.

"You Mr. Kalensky?" a middle-aged man jumped out of the car to ask.

"That's right." Cas handed over the luggage and turned to grab Lisel's other suitcase from her unresisting hands.

Once their luggage had been stowed in the limo's roomy trunk and they were under way, the driver asked, "How was your flight?"

"Long," Cas briefly retorted.

The driver threw his riders a wary look in the rearview mirror and flipped on the radio, filling the back seat with soothing Muzak. They made it down the length of the Kennedy Expressway without more than a dozen words being said and a majority of those were directions to Lisel's apartment.

A uniformed doorman stood waiting to open the limo's door once it had pulled to a halt outside the awninged entrance of her apartment building. "Thanks for the ride," Lisel coolly stated.

"Wait." Cas's hand on her arm kept her by his side. "Lisel, we have to talk. Have dinner with me."

"I'm not hungry."

"Then let's go somewhere for coffee. I think we need to talk, don't you?"

"Yes." They needed to talk about what was happening to them, why the teasing lover she'd known in the Alps had changed into this semistranger.

"Fine. Then leave your luggage with the doorman. We'll go drop off my stuff, and then we'll go somewhere quiet and talk."

The "somewhere quiet" turned out to be a small coffeehouse.

Cupping her hands around a cup of mocha special blend, Lisel prompted him. "You were awfully quiet on the plane. Is something wrong?"

Had Cas been looking at her, he would have seen the way she directed her question to his right shoulder instead of to his face. But Cas was also guilty of avoiding direct visual contact as he stirred sugar into his espresso. He also avoided a direct answer to her question by saying, "You weren't exactly talkative yourself, you know."

"I was thinking."

"About what?"

"About a lot of things." She shrugged. "What about you?"

"I was thinking, too."

She repeated his question. "About what?"

"I think you know."

Lisel shook her head. "Why don't you tell me?"

At that point a third voice broke into their discussion.

"Would you two like refills?" their cheerful waitress inquired.

"No," Cas said, adding a belated "thanks."

"Just give me a call if you need anything. My name's Wanda."

"We'll do that," Cas assured her, willing Wanda to disappear.

She did, but only after asking again if they needed anything. As soon as Wanda left, Lisel resumed their discussion where it had left off, with her suggesting, "Why don't you tell me what you were thinking about?"

"About us." He set down his coffee cup. "That's what you were thinking about, too, wasn't it?" His inflection turned the question into a statement.

Lisel didn't deny it. "When we got on the plane, something changed." *Tell me I'm imagining things,* her heart implored.

Cas's explanation was disturbingly logical. "We were coming back to reality."

The premonition of impending disaster rose like a scream within her. All this talk about reality . . . she could see where it was heading. And that vision hurt her more than anything had ever hurt her before. Determined not to let him know the true depth of her pain, she agreed. "The time we spent together in the Alps was like a dream."

"It *did* seem like a dream," he said.

Striving to sound rational, she pointed out, "The problem with dreams is that you have to wake up."

"True, but where does that leave us?"

"I'm not sure," she replied, confusion clouding her face. *How could things go wrong so quickly?*

"I'm not sure either." Cas shoved aside his cup of espresso as if irritated by its very existence. "Did you mean what you said about loving me, or was that all part of the dream?" he abruptly demanded.

Unprepared to leave herself wide open for rejection, she countered, "What about you? Did you mean it when you said you loved me?"

Cas's affirmative nod was ruined by his qualifying words. "I meant it at the time."

Lisel felt as though she'd had the rug pulled out from under her. "What does that mean?" she cried.

"It means that maybe we were carried away by the passion of the moment. You read about these things happening all the time. Two people meet on vacation, and because they're relaxed and having a good time in a romantic location, they think they're in love."

"I spent the entire summer in that romantic location without thinking I was falling in love. Until you came along." This was as close as Lisel could come to announcing her feelings out loud.

His response hit her as forcibly as a slap on the face. "Well, however it happened, we are back in reality now, and we both have a lot of thinking to do. I feel it might be a good idea if we did that thinking and held off seeing each other for a while."

Oh, my God! He is breaking it off! Lisel immediately retreated behind a shell, using her drink as a shield. She took a few refined sips before saying, "I agree." Her inflection was deliberately blank; her features were schooled to indifference. "After all, I'm going to be starting my new job in a few days, and that will be taking up a lot of my time." She even managed to inject a note of professional enthusiasm in her voice.

"And I'll no doubt find a mountain of work waiting for me at the bank," Cas remarked in a like manner.

Silence stretched between them as Cas took care of the bill and escorted Lisel outside.

94

She regarded him coolly. "If you don't mind, I think I'll catch a cab and go home. My inner clock is still on European time."

"I'll call you," Cas said.

To Lisel his words were an empty promise, lightly made and not intended to be kept. Therefore, she didn't even bother acknowledging them. With a hurried "good-bye" she hailed a conveniently cruising cab and closed the door on a chapter of her life.

CHAPTER SIX

When will you learn? Lisel asked herself as she dumped her luggage inside her subleased apartment. She was too tired to fight the self-recriminating lecture her mind was bent on delivering.

What did you expect? There were no promises of commitment given. You should have been more cautious. You should have foreseen this, instead of wearing romantic rose-colored glasses. You should have known better!

Her twenty-twenty hindsight was blurred by tears. The pain of rejection tore through her with the devastation of a metal claw. Just when the bruised roots of her self-esteem had begun to grow again, they were delivered another crushing blow.

Lisel swiped an angry hand at her wet cheeks. First Rick and now this. Damn all men! Cas didn't deserve her love, and he wasn't worth her tears. He'd obviously never loved her. It had all been an illusion—passionate and romantic, but dispensable. That realization served only to increase her tears.

Hoping to improve her shattered spirits, Lisel moved

over to an array of expensive hi-fi equipment and flicked on a switch that filled the room with music. Unfortunately the song was about love gone wrong. She switched off the stereo receiver with a vehemence frowned upon by the manufacturer. Lisel sniffed inelegantly, too depressed to get a Kleenex.

The city lights, displayed by the living room's generous expanse of plate glass, beckoned to her. She stared out into the darkness, past her tearstained reflection. Some knight in shining armor Cas had turned out to be. How could he do this to her?

"Very easily," she answered herself, wiping away the tears with the back of her hand. Right now she just wanted to climb into bed and pull the covers over her head. But most of all, she wanted to forget she'd ever heard of Cas Kalensky.

During the next few days Lisel tried very hard to do just that. She needed a morale boost and wanted a new look. Going shopping seemed the lesser of two evils when the other choice was having her hair shorn short! So she ended up settling for a new wardrobe of fall suits instead, spending all day Saturday at Chicago's exclusive Water Tower Place and making the most of the preseason sales.

By Monday morning the woman who faced her in the mirror looked light-years apart from the relaxed Lisel she'd been in Austria. The natural beauty of her eyes was accentuated by the skillful use of makeup. A brocade cream blouse tastefully set off her new navy blue suit. With her hair left loose but scrupulously pulled away from her face, she looked the epitome of a successful businesswoman.

After braving the rush of Monday morning crowds clogging the buses and jamming the streets, Lisel arrived at the fourth-floor offices of Linguistics Incorporated at precisely 9:00 A.M.

97

"My name is Lisel Mayer—"

"And you're our newest interpreter," the Chinese receptionist inserted. "Hi. I'm Kim Chang, Reuben Leibman's secretary. Reuben's asked me to show you around. As you'll soon see, our offices aren't very large, so this shouldn't take long!"

Lisel welcomed Kim's open friendliness, responding with a matching warmth. "Thanks."

"You may not be thanking me when you see the pile of work left on your desk. Ron, the guy who had the German division before you, has set up a full week's worth of appointments for you, starting this afternoon with a Swiss tool and die manufacturer in town for the convention at McCormick Place."

Throughout the next few days Kim's friendliness made Lisel's transition into the office a much smoother experience. The workload was heavy; the number of employees small. Besides herself there were two other interpreters, one for Spanish and one for Japanese. The Latin-based languages of French and Italian as well as the Arabic languages were handled by Linguistics Incorporated's director, Reuben Leibman. In all, Reuben spoke seven languages fluently. Lisel had yet to label all seven, but she did know that German was among them.

At the end of her first week Kim took Lisel out to lunch for a real gabfest at a nearby salad bar. "Well?" Kim demanded as they stood with plates in hand. "What do you think so far?"

Lisel eyed the vast array of salads and toppings. "The selection is really extensive."

"I wasn't asking about the salad bar. I meant the office. What do you think?"

"I've been there only a week," Lisel cautiously replied.

"And?" Kim prompted, adding an extra dollop of blue cheese dressing to her romaine lettuce.

"And I like it."

"Despite Reuben's germ phobia?"

Lisel laughed at Kim's descriptive phrasing. "I can't believe he makes you spray his phone with disinfectant every morning."

"If you find that hard to believe, you'd really freak out if you ever rode with Reuben on the elevator."

"Why's that?" Lisel questioned, following Kim's pilgrimage toward a free table.

"He doesn't breathe."

"You're kidding!"

"I'm not," Kim denied, sliding into the booth. "He holds his breath for fear he'll inhale germs. It's a good thing our office is only on the fourth floor, or he'd be in trouble!"

Lisel cracked up, almost choking on her bean sprouts.

"It's good to see you laughing," Kim noted.

"Have I been that grim?"

"Not really. And God knows that Reuben would be enough to send anyone over the deep end!"

For all her complaining, Lisel knew that Kim was fond of her eccentric boss. But it was a fondness tempered with occasional flares of impatience, as Lisel found out when they returned to the office.

"Where have you been?" Reuben demanded in a demented fashion.

Kim, unimpressed by her boss's frantic demeanor, retorted, "At lunch." Her dark eyes reflected impatience. "I told you where we were going when Lisel and I left."

Reuben ignored her comment. "I can't find the Hinkler file, and he's due to arrive here in precisely four minutes."

Kim reached over and plucked the missing item from the top of her desk. "It's right here."

Reuben addressed his next question to Lisel. "Where are you going?"

Safely out of Reuben's view, Kim rolled her eyes in exasperation while Lisel replied, "I'm going back to my office."

"Forget it. Hinkler is your next assignment."

Lisel frowned in confusion. "He's not listed on the roster." She'd checked her assignment book before going to lunch.

"I know that. It's a last-minute arrangement, but he's willing to pay well for our services." Further explanation was precluded by the client's arrival. "Ah, Herr Hinkler." Reuben greeted him in German, leading the stocky businessman into his office and inquiring about his flight. After the polite exchange Reuben went on to introduce Lisel.

Herr Hinkler briskly shook her hand while stating in a clipped High German, "We must hurry, or I will be late for my appointment."

Lisel found herself rushed out of the office and into the elevator before she could frame a reply. This was ridiculous! How could she even hail a cab if she didn't know where they were going? Grabbing the opportunity provided by the elevator ride, she asked Herr Hinkler where his appointment was.

"First American Bank."

Lisel swallowed a ripple of panic as she tried to remember where Cas worked. It was one of Chicago's major banks, but which one? First American, First Continental, First Federal, First National? She didn't have a clue!

She was still searching her memory when they walked into First American's award-winning structure. They were directed to the fourteenth floor and an empty conference room. After waiting for five minutes, Herr Hinkler demanded that Lisel go find out what was causing the delay.

"Excuse me," she requested of the receptionist who had seated them in the conference room.

"Yes?"

"Will the wait be much longer?"

"No, it shouldn't be. Mr. Kalensky is on his way down."

"Kalensky?" she repeated in shocked dismay, having convinced herself that he must work at the First National. "Not Cas Kalensky?"

"That's right. Do you know him?"

Without a conscious decision on her part, Lisel found herself shaking her head.

"Don't look so worried, dear," the older woman advised solicitously. "You'll like Mr. Kalensky. He's a nice man—a bit too serious at times . . ."

Cas? Serious? Lisel shook her head again, this time in disbelief.

". . . but then these economists are like that, aren't they?" the receptionist blithely continued. "Anyway, there's no need to look so worried," she added, noting Lisel's expression. "I'm sure Mr. Kalensky won't bite you."

No, but I'd sure like to take a few bites out of him, Lisel malevolently thought.

"Is something wrong?" the receptionist asked, wary of the storm signals she'd seen in Lisel's eyes.

"No, nothing." Lisel strove to get her emotions under control before returning to the conference room and Herr Hinkler.

Both her expression and her German were professional. "The bank official will be here shortly."

And he was. Had Lisel passed Cas on the street, she probably wouldn't have recognized him. Hadn't he once teasingly told her that she wouldn't know him dressed in a business suit? But it wasn't merely the impeccable lines of the formal business attire that threw her off guard. It was the presence of a pair of studious-looking glasses that

101

changed the lines of his face, making him appear austere and unapproachable.

Cas's brown eyes reflected the same startled quality as hers. What was Lisel doing here? And with Hinkler, of all people. His gaze rapidly assessed her from the crown of her loose honey brown hair, over the feminine curves hidden by her suit jacket, and down the length of her nylon-clad legs. She looked different, more . . . professional was the only word that came to mind, but it didn't fully describe the change. Besides the new maturity to her demeanor, there was a certain cynicism reflected in the cool depths of her eyes and in the empty politeness of her smile.

Having had some amount of advance warning, Lisel had her own emotions firmly under control. "Mr. Kalensky? I'm Lisel Mayer, Herr Hinkler's interpreter."

"I see." Cas had recovered himself, his voice impassive as he stated, "The bank has its own interpreters, Ms. Mayer. Mr. Hinkler didn't have to go to the expense of hiring one himself. Please inform him that I'll have an in-house interpreter assigned to our meetings beginning tomorrow."

Her eyes darkened with repressed fury. Not only had he broken her heart, but now he was trying to interfere with her clients. Throwing Cas a withering look that was sure to penetrate his glasses, she firmly said, "There's no need for that. Herr Hinkler has chosen to hire me as his interpreter."

"Perhaps he was unaware of the bank's own interpreting services, in which case I feel that you should inform him of our willingness to supply an interpreter at no cost to him. And since Mr. Hinkler has come to inquire about a loan from our bank, I would think cost efficiency is important to him, wouldn't you?"

Telling herself that kicking Cas would serve no good purpose, Lisel had to settle for letting her eyes do the talking. They stated her opinion eloquently before she abruptly turned to inform Herr Hinkler of this latest development. He didn't look overly thrilled at the prospect of a new interpreter, but he made no protest.

"Well?" Cas pursued the point.

"Herr Hinkler is agreeable to using your interpreter for future discussions, but he wishes to retain me for today's meeting. It would save time."

Cas didn't approve of her involvement, even for one day, but he couldn't find a logical reason to insist on her immediate removal. With a cool smile and a nod he instructed, "Please relay my apologies to Mr. Hinkler. I'm sorry I'm late, I was unavoidably detained."

Lisel relayed the message, shortening Cas's apology in the translation. Herr Hinkler waved it aside with a man-to-man joviality that set her teeth on edge. When he lit a thick cigar a few minutes later, she gritted her already beleaguered teeth and didn't voice an objection until the smoke got so bad that her stomach revolted. Even then her request that he stop smoking was softly and politely worded.

Herr Hinkler was indifferent to her discomfort. "Smoking helps my concentration," he said in German.

Cas eyed Lisel's unnaturally pale features and then shoved an ashtray across the polished expanse of the conference table. Pointing to the rank cigar, he concisely stated, *"Verboten."* His impatient finger pointed to the "No smoking" sign displayed on the far wall. Lisel watched in angry disbelief as Herr Hinkler immediately extinguished the cigar, even going so far as to smile apologetically. Men! After she had allowed herself one brief moment of feminine disgust, her self-control didn't slip again during the remainder of the afternoon.

Cas could find no fault with her linguistic skills. Aside from the slashing glare she'd sent him following the cigar incident, her face reflected no emotion as she handled the translations between English and German with smooth efficiency.

It was nearing five before Cas called a halt to the discussions. Once they had gathered their notes together, the two men shook hands. Lisel was preparing to accompany Herr Hinkler out of the conference room when Cas commanded, "I'd like to see you in my office, Ms. Mayer."

"I'm afraid that's impossible," she replied. "I've got to see that Herr Hinkler gets back to his hotel."

"I'll have someone else take care of that." Cas quickly delegated the task to the receptionist. Taking Lisel by the arm, he said, "You come with me." He escorted her down the hallway in the manner of a guard escorting a prisoner. His secretary looked on in surprise at the sight of her normally imperturbable boss dragging an attractive woman into his office.

Cas slammed the door, indifferent to the speculation his behavior was arousing in the outer office. He stood with his back to the door, blocking her means of escape. Lisel jerked her arm out of his grasp. "You really should be grateful," he had the nerve to say.

"Grateful," she echoed, her expression one of incredulous amazement. "How do you figure that?"

Cas shoved his glasses up over his forehead until they were perched atop his head. He immediately appeared more approachable and therefore more dangerous. "I've relieved you of a cigar-smoking industrialist."

"How self-sacrificing of you." Her marveling tone was wrapped in sarcasm. "But you really needn't have put yourself out on my account. There's no reason why I can't continue as Herr Hinkler's translator."

"No way!" Cas was adamant.

"Why?" she bluntly demanded.

He inhaled deeply, obviously striving for patience. "I've already told you. The bank has its own interpreters."

"Then why are we having this discussion?"

He abandoned the search for patience and got right to the point. "What do you mean by acting as if you don't know me?"

So that's why he'd used the strong-arm tactics. Dented male pride. "What did you want me to say," she hissed, anger flushing her cheeks, " 'Here's the man I made the mistake of sleeping with once upon a time'?"

"It wasn't a mistake, and it wasn't once upon a time. It was only a week ago."

She nonchalantly strolled over to the window and made a pretense of checking the view. "A week ago?" The words were murmured with mocking indifference. "Is that all it's been? Strange how time flies when you're having fun."

"Why are you putting on this act?" he demanded, infuriated by her cool self-possession.

"Act?" Her control snapped. She whirled to face him, fury marking her inflection. "You're a fine one to talk about acting. I think your performance in the Alps deserves an Oscar."

Cas made a mocking bow. "I'm glad to hear my performance pleased you."

Lisel gasped at his audacity. "I'm not even going to dignify that with an answer."

"I've tried calling you all week, and you haven't been home." The downward slant of his mouth signaled his displeasure.

"That's right," she distantly acknowledged. "I've been out."

"Every night?" His voice rose to a bellow.

Outside, his secretary eyed the closed door of his office in alarm. Mr. Kalensky never bellowed! "There must be a full moon or something," she muttered while gathering her personal belongings. It was after five, and she was leaving. The coolly unforgiving mood her boss had been in all week lent wings to her feet as she made her departure.

Meanwhile, inside the office the fight continued. "What are you?" Lisel flared. "My keeper?"

"No." His response was immediate. "I'm your lover."

"Former lover," Lisel corrected. Panicked because he'd left his post at the door and was moving in on her, she used words to keep him at bay. "One-night stand actually comes a little closer to the truth."

The fury written on Cas's face warned Lisel that she'd better get out of harm's way while she still had the chance. Deserting the field of battle was out of character for her, but self-preservation was her primary goal!

Using a clever side step she'd perfected while playing high school basketball, she was out the door and on her way to the elevator before Cas could make a move to stop her. Thankfully the elevator doors stood open, waiting to whisk her away. She raced inside, pivoting to jab impatiently the button marked "Lobby."

"Come on. Come on," she muttered, willing the doors to close. They eventually did, but not before a furious Cas had slipped between them.

"I'm not done talking to you yet," he growled as the doors slid shut.

Before she could make an appropriately stinging rejoinder, the elevator abruptly ground to a halt, and the interior lights went out, plunging them in darkness. Lisel instinctively grabbed for Cas. His arms protectively encircled her until common sense reasserted itself. What was she doing? Cas was no longer her knight in shining armor. Why was she looking to him for rescue?

As she freed herself and stood upright, another possibility occurred to her. "Did you do something to make the elevator stop?" she suspiciously demanded.

"Me?"

"I don't see anyone else in here."

"I fail to comprehend how you can *see* anything in here," Cas muttered.

"But then I wouldn't say comprehension was one of your strong points," Lisel nastily retorted. "What did you do to the elevator?"

"Nothing."

"Oh." She didn't sound as certain of herself now. Besides, her fear of the dark was beginning to make itself felt. It was black as pitch; she literally couldn't see her hand in front of her face. "In that case, what happened?"

"How should I know?"

"You work here," she snapped, determined to use anger as a shield. "Do something."

"I'm an economist, not an elevator boy."

"You're not a boy at all," she sniped.

"How kind of you to notice," he drawled.

"Don't you have a light? A book of matches or something?"

"No. Don't you?"

"No." She sensed his movement in the inky darkness. "Where are you going?"

"Not very far, obviously," he mocked. "I'm just trying to find the elevator phone. Damn!" he muttered.

"What happened?"

"I just tripped over something."

"It was probably my purse. I dropped it when the elevator stopped."

"That figures. Ah, I found it." She heard the sound of him dialing. "Security? This is Cas Kalensky. There are two of us stuck in elevator number three. The mechanism stopped, and the lights went dead. What's the problem?"

107

Although Lisel heard the faint murmur of a voice through the amplification of the receiver, she couldn't distinguish any of the words.

"I see. And how long will that take?" Cas asked. There was a pause while he waited for an answer. "Okay. Thanks." He hung up, cursing under his breath as his finger got caught between the receiver and the wall unit.

"Well?" Lisel prodded. "What's wrong?"

"Something to do with the traffic lights being downed in an accident and the electricity in the entire block being switched off while they clear the street of the live wires."

"How long will that take?"

"They thought no longer than thirty minutes."

"Isn't there an emergency generator? The building can't just go without electricity." Visions of million-dollar heists filled her mind. "This is a bank!"

"You're absolutely correct." He congratulated her, as if she'd just made a brilliant discovery. "This is a bank. And there is an emergency generator . . ."

"Well, then?" she interjected.

". . . which is used to power the security system and the computer room," he went on to say, "not the elevators."

"So we're cooped up in here for the next half hour?"

"Looks that way," he agreed. "You're not afraid, are you?"

"Is there any reason why I should be?"

"No. But I know that you don't care for the dark. I remember that trip up to Moserboden—"

Lisel interrupted his reminiscences by tartly instructing him, "Don't bother."

She heard his sigh. "We're going to be here for a while. We might as well make ourselves comfortable."

"And how do you propose we do that?"

This time she heard the rustle of clothing. What was Cas doing? Wild possibilities occurred to her.

"Before you get hysterical," Cas mocked, "let me assure you that I am only removing my jacket so we can sit on it. Ah." He sighed a moment later. "That's better. Are you going to join me?"

Lisel carefully weighed her options, which boiled down to either standing there like a martyr or joining him. Her feet, cramped in their new shoes, made the decision for her. Sitting, even next to Cas, was preferable to standing. "Yes, I'll join you."

Unable to see his helping hand, she bumped into it on her way down. To make matters worse, she ended up sitting more on Cas than on his jacket! In her hurry to remove herself to a more decorous position, her hand inadvertently brushed against his upper thigh. Her fingers registered the rippling strength beneath the gabardine material of his slacks before she snatched them away.

Inwardly cursing her fumbling clumsiness, she blocked out the lingering warmth of the unexpectedly intimate contact and politely apologized. "I'm sorry."

"So am I," he surprised her by saying. "Sorry I spewed all that garbage at you."

"Are you referring to the knock-down, drag-out fight we had in your office?"

"No, I'm referring to the talk we had when we got back from the Alps."

"Oh. That talk."

"I don't know what came over me, but one thing I do know. I love you."

CHAPTER SEVEN

"Did you hear me?" Cas questioned. "I said I love you."

"I heard you," Lisel acknowledged, her voice flat.

"Well?"

"Well, what?"

"Aren't you going to say anything?"

"What is there to say?" she countered.

"That you love me, too."

"I don't."

There was a moment of stunned disbelief before Cas protested, "You can't fall out of love in a week."

"Why not?" she retorted, her inflection even and unemotional. "I fell *in* love in a week."

"Lisel, we've got something special. Let's not throw it away."

"You should've thought of that sooner."

"Are you trying to punish me, is that it?"

"No," she wearily answered. "I'm not out to hurt you. I'm just trying to prevent myself from getting hurt."

"I want to see you again," Cas stated.

"To use your own words—'No way!' "

"Everyone's entitled to one mistake in this life," he said, almost to himself, "and mine was letting you go."

"You didn't let me go," Lisel corrected him. "You dumped me. There is a difference!"

"I can understand your anger—"

"Can you?" she interrupted. "I wonder how you'd like to be left high and dry."

"I didn't leave you high and dry," Cas protested.

"No? What would you call it?"

"Cold feet," he bluntly confessed.

She was unimpressed with his candor. "I see. And how do I know that this malady isn't going to recur?"

"Because I love you."

"Did you love me when you got cold feet before?"

He stiffened as he realized, too late, where her line of questioning was going. "Yes, but—"

"Then I'd say that love doesn't seem to afford much protection," she ruthlessly concluded.

With a growled "You're *saying* entirely too much!" Cas's hand snaked out to clamp over her mouth. Lisel's protesting squirming was expediently brought to a halt by a restraining arm that wedged her between its steely warmth and the elevator wall.

"I realize this is hard to understand . . ." he began with deliberate patience.

"That's putting it mildly," she muttered against his hand, furious at the shards of awareness piercing her control.

". . . but it's also hard for me to explain. Now are you going to sit there and argue, or are you going to listen to me?"

He removed his hand only long enough for her to voice an answer. "Sit here and argue."

His sigh was clearly audible through the inky darkness, his exhalation of breath stirring the tendrils of hair curling

111

over her temple. Lisel's already churning emotions took another somersault, and her number one priority became gaining some distance from Cas. Tugging his hand away, she relented. "I'll listen—provided you keep your hands off me."

She was released with some measure of reluctance. Cas had missed holding her in his arms, missed touching her. He had to bridge the rift he'd created. He'd known it wouldn't be easy; Lisel wasn't the sort of woman to enter lightly into the intimacies they'd shared. But he was just coming to realize how difficult his quest would be. She'd erected her defenses with implacable will, and it would take unfailing determination on his part to bridge those defenses.

"I was attracted to you from the first moment I laid eyes on you," he assured her. "You were attracted, too. I could see it in your eyes. There were no flirtatious protests, no games. You'd been hurt, I could see that. You were reluctant to get involved. I understood that. But, honey, there was magic between us." His voice reached out to stroke her as his hands couldn't. "Coming back to the reality of Chicago was a shock. I didn't know if the magic could survive. I thought we both needed time. Time to sift through the magic and find the facts. The fact was that I'd done more than *fall* in love with you. I loved you. Plain and simple. But there was nothing plain and simple about the way I felt. On the contrary, it seemed complicated and scary as hell. What I'm trying to say is this: Being in love can be frightening, and sometimes it's easier to fight it than it is to face it."

His explanation affected her; there was no denying that. But she was only too aware of the damage Cas had inflicted on her already shattered self-respect. She simply couldn't take another chance; the risk factor was too high. "Cas, I appreciate your trying to explain things to me, but

I really think it would be best if we didn't go into this. It's over."

His challenge was immediate. "Kiss me and then tell me it's over."

She struggled to her feet. "Forget it!" Her rejection was a tad too vehement.

Cas rose to join her. "What's the problem?" A steady calmness marked his inflection. "If you're over what you felt for me, as you claim to be, then kissing me without emotion would prove it."

"This isn't a trial," she scoffed. "I don't have to prove anything. And I never claimed that the physical attraction between us was dead."

"Then we'll begin with that."

Lisel opened her mouth to make a sharp retort, but it was stolen from her as he captured her parted lips. Cas gave her no chance for retreat, his powerful body riveting her to the elevator wall. Yet for all his aggression, he wasn't savage with her. That was neither his style nor his intention.

Instead his mouth courted hers with arousing insistence, his every action embroidered with sensual intimacy. No portion of her mouth was left unexplored. The inverted curve of her upper lip was propositioned with ravishing nibbles. The fleshy inner sheathing of her lower lip was painted with the tip of his tongue, the evocative brush-strokes creating a feathery caress that was passion-provoking. Finally, the honeyed warmth within was explored with hungry tenderness.

Tasting her response, Cas boldly pulled her closer. Their mouths melded together, her tongue answering the thrusting parry of his. He seemed to have perfect recall, his hands seeking out her pleasure points as if it had been minutes instead of days since he'd caressed them.

They both were breathless by the time his mouth left

113

hers to voyage across her cheek, temporarily coming to rest at her temple. "Doesn't this tell you something?" he rasped.

"That I should stay away from you," she shakily responded.

His hand curved over her cheek with tender protectiveness. "I'm not going to hurt you."

"That's right. You're not." She eased herself away from him. "Because I don't intend to let you get close enough."

"I'll prove it to you," he vowed. "I'm going to court you so relentlessly that you won't be able to resist me."

"You'll be wasting your time."

"Why don't you let me be the judge of that?"

"Because you're not acting very judiciously."

He aimed a gentle kiss toward the tip of her nose. "Love does that to people."

As suddenly as it had gone out, the power started up again. Lisel and Cas stepped apart, blinking owlishly at the sudden surge of illumination after their extended period of darkness.

"I'll give you a lift home," Cas stated as the elevator smoothly resumed its descent.

"I can take a cab."

He punched the underground garage button. "I know you can, but you don't have to."

"I'd prefer it."

"You'd prefer to stand outside in a downpour? Why? Not afraid to be with me, are you?"

"I'd rather not answer that question, on the ground that I might incriminate myself."

The elevator doors slid open as he promised, "I'll be on my best behavior. Scout's honor."

"Swear on a stack of *Fortune* magazines," she dryly suggested, "and maybe I'll believe you."

After taking her by the elbow, Cas guided her over to

114

a red luxury sedan. "I'll go one step further and swear on the hood of my BMW that I'll behave. For tonight," he qualified, unlocking the passenger door and holding it open invitingly. "Come on. Hop in."

"All right." Lisel relented, getting into the car. "I wasn't far off when I guessed you drove a Mercedes," she found herself saying as he swung the car out of his reserved parking space. To cover up her unintended reference to the past, she sarcastically inquired, "Aren't you afraid that I'll go after you because of your money?"

Cas shot her an indulgent look. "Are you going after me?"

"No."

"Then I've got nothing to fear." His shrug drew her attention to the powerful breadth of his shoulders.

"Maybe I'm just playing hard to get," she perversely pointed out.

"If so, you can quit playing," he calmly informed her. "I'll catch you in the end."

Her fingers curled into the expensive leather seat. "Sure of yourself, aren't you?"

"I'm sure of the way I feel about you."

"You weren't before," she shot back.

"As I said, everyone is entitled to one mistake. Having second thoughts about us was mine." Pausing to insert his ID card into the parking security slot, Cas drawled, "I may be dumb, but I'm not stupid."

"How did you arrive at that brilliant conclusion?"

His gaze touched her across the confined width of the car. "Because I'm not about to let stubborn pride stand in the way of our future together."

"I am not stubborn!"

"Of course not," he indulgently agreed, pulling into traffic.

Deciding it was time to change the subject, she said, "I never knew you wore glasses."

"I only wear them when I'm working."

"Part and parcel of your banker's image?" she sarcastically suggested.

A red light gave Cas the opportunity to turn his head and study her. A moment later he smiled and said, "It isn't going to work, you know."

"If you're talking about resuming our affair, then you're right. It isn't going to work."

"Our relationship does work. The kiss in the elevator already established that. I was referring to the fact that I'm on to you now. You're not going to make me lose my temper."

"I have no idea what you're talking about," she distantly informed him.

"I'm talking about your obvious attempts to make me angry, so that I'll say something to fuel your own anger toward me. That's what you pulled in my office when you claimed I was a one-night stand." He waited for a confirmation or a denial. When he received neither, he calmly continued. "I'm just letting you know that it won't work again. Thought I'd save you the trouble of trying to incur my wrath because it won't work. I have no intention of messing up again."

"Meaning you did mess up before?"

"Yes," he readily admitted as the light turned green.

Lisel tried to figure out his angle. Why was he so determined? "Listen, if you're suffering from a guilty conscience or something, forget it. Life goes on. I'm not about to do something desperate. So let's just drop the whole thing, okay?"

Cas shook his head. "Not okay. Honey, I love you. And I'm going to keep on telling you that until you believe it."

After sniping, "You could be retirement age by then!",

116

she stubbornly remained silent for the remainder of the trip. Cas already knew where she lived, so there was no need to give him directions.

"I'll see you to your door," he stated, getting out of the car and following her inside.

"You don't have to do that. We have a very capable doorman." The uniformed attendant stood right before them, all six and a half feet, 250 pounds of him! Lisel made the introductions with a triumphant smile. "Arnie, this is Cas Kalensky. He's concerned about my safety. Why don't you reassure him on that score while I go on upstairs? Good night, Cas." Nodding politely, she left him in Arnie's more than capable burly hands.

Lisel squarely placed the blame for her restless, half-sleepless night on Cas's doorstep. Regardless of how many times she tried shoving them aside, thoughts of him kept crowding her mind. Even as she dressed for work the next morning, his image was still persistently present and was responsible for the run in her new pair of textured stockings as well as the tea stain on her favorite blouse. The prospect of having to tell Reuben that she'd lost a client provided additional fuel to her already bad temper.

Things weren't improved any by her having to stand during the entire sardine-packed twenty-minute bus ride to the office. By the time she arrived at work, the tweed blazer, tailored cinnamon shirt, and trim-fitting black wool skirt she wore all felt as if she'd slept in them.

"What are you doing here?" Reuben demanded.

"Good morning, Lisel." Kim's friendly greeting was meant to mock Reuben's hassled abruptness.

"Lisel, I think we'd better talk in my office," Reuben officiously stated.

She followed him into his office, silently cursing Cas for putting her in this unenviable position.

117

"You're supposed to be with Herr Hinkler," Reuben said in the manner of one reminding a forgetful relative.

Lisel gratefully sank onto the chair he offered her. "I ran into a slight problem."

"Not wandering hands again?"

"No!" She'd had that problem with only one client, Fritz Schultz, an inveterate pincher. "Nothing like that. The bank preferred to use its own interpreters."

Reuben frowned across the desk at her. "Why?"

"Why?" she repeated blankly.

"It's a simple enough question."

"Mr. Kalensky stated that it would be more economical to use their own staff than for Herr Hinkler to expend additional funds of his own," she repeated as if by rote.

"Who's this Kalensky character?"

"A financial adviser at the bank."

Reuben stroked his chin and murmured, "Strange . . ."

"What's strange?"

"We've provided occasional interpreting services for that bank before, and they never called in their own people." He dropped his meditative pose and briskly said, "It's just as well, I suppose."

"It is?" Lisel stared at him in bewilderment.

"I did some checking into Hinkler's background. You know we're generally pretty particular about our clients here at Linguistics. After all, we have a reputation to protect."

Really, why couldn't Reuben get to the point? Getting information out of him was worse than pulling teeth. Pulling teeth . . . She absently rubbed her lower jaw, where a molar sent out a painful twinge every now and then. She'd have to see about getting to a dentist sometime, maybe in a month or two. Shaking off that unsettling prospect, she returned to the matter at hand. "Did you discover something unsatisfactory about Herr Hinkler?"

"Nothing concrete, but several unsavory suspicions."

"What type of suspicions?"

From Reuben's manner Lisel expected to hear tales of white slavery or drug trafficking at the very least. Instead he said, "Questionable business practices. But then most international companies are guilty of that."

She didn't care what most international companies did. She didn't even care what Herr Hinkler did. But she did wonder if Cas was aware of Hinkler's reputation. Of course, he must be. That was his job. Just as interpreting was her job, as long as overbearing economists didn't steal her clients away!

Even though Reuben had taken Hinkler's loss well, it still rankled her that Cas had removed her as the interpreter on the account. Was he one of those men who felt threatened by a capable woman? Lisel shook her head, answering her own question. He hadn't been threatened by her mastery of German when they'd been in the Alps. In fact, he'd welcomed her as his guide, depended upon her.

She couldn't figure it out, and just trying gave her a headache.

"Are you all right?" Kim asked in concern, watching her friend's weary departure from Reuben's office. "Did Reuben upset you?"

"No."

"Well, something's bothering you. Want to talk about it?"

"I'd rather hit it over the head!" Lisel's muttered comment wasn't meant to be overheard.

Kim, however, prided herself on her acute hearing and sensitive perception. "What's his name?" she conversationally inquired.

119

Lisel blinked in surprise. "Whose name?"

"This guy you want to hit over the head."

"Cas Kalensky."

"Who's he?"

"A financial adviser at the bank. He dismissed me as Herr Hinkler's interpreter, said he preferred to use an in-house interpreter."

A summons from Reuben prevented Kim from pursuing the subject. "We'll talk at lunch," she said with an indulgent grimace at her boss's raised voice.

They resumed their conversation exactly where they'd left off. "So who is this Cas Kalensky?" Kim demanded as they stood in line at their now regular lunch site, the Let Us Eat Salad Bar.

"I already told you."

"Only the dry details. Now tell me the juicy stuff!"

"What makes you think there is any juicy stuff?" Lisel countered.

"Those dark circles under your eyes."

"All right." Lisel sighed. "Let me load my plate in peace, and then I'll tell you some of the juicy stuff."

Once ensconced in a quiet corner booth, Lisel related a sketchy outline of her relationship with Cas. "We met in Austria. You know I spent this past summer there with a cousin of mine. They ran a hotel, and Cas was a guest. We got very close. I loved him, and Cas said he loved me. But when we flew back to Chicago together, he suddenly became withdrawn and taciturn."

"What happened?"

"I don't know. When we met again at the bank, Cas was furious because I acted as if I didn't know him. We got stuck in an elevator—"

"Stuck in an elevator!"

Lisel waved away that part of her narrative as being

120

irrelevant. "Anyway, that's when Cas claimed he got cold feet. Now he wants to resume our relationship."

"He actually admitted getting cold feet?" Kim asked in surprise. At Lisel's nod, she mused, "Sounds like the honest type to me."

"Honest!" Lisel stabbed a tomato slice with undue force. "Why did he have to get cold feet in Chicago? Why not Austria?"

"*Mmm.*" Kim paused to swallow her slice of avocado. "That's part of what I call the shipboard romance syndrome."

"Do go on, Dr. Chang."

Kim grinned at Lisel's mocking invitation. "All right, I will. It's a well-known fact that people act differently on vacation. Away from the pressures of daily living you can become someone else. Aren't you a different woman from the Lisel you were in Austria?"

"Yes."

"And I'm willing to bet that Cas is also different."

"Very much so. In Austria he was fun-loving, tender, and passionate. He wore jeans and taught me how to ski. Now he's a hard-boiled, conventional economist in a three-piece suit. Which is the real Cas?"

"Probably a combination of both."

"In your discourse on the shipboard romance syndrome, you neglected to address the inevitable conclusion. Reality supersedes romance, and suddenly"—Lisel snapped her fingers—"it's all over!"

"But you said Cas wanted to start again," Kim pointed out.

"Yes. I can't imagine why," she bitterly retorted.

"Look in a mirror. Blue-eyed blondes are always popular."

"My hair isn't blonde; it's brown. And my eyes aren't exactly blue either."

121

Kim waved her breadstick and declared, "Details, mere details. Back to the main topic of our discussion—Cas Kalensky. What's he like?"

"Impossible!"

"There must be something about him that attracted you. Aha, I can tell by that dreamy look in your eyes that there was more than just something."

"The Cas I fell in love with was able to laugh at himself because he was self-confident enough to know what he wanted and to go after it."

"Ah, I get it. By falling victim to a case of cold feet, your hero developed feet of clay."

"What's that supposed to mean?"

"It means that Cas was no longer the swashbuckling hero who swept you off your feet in the Alps. Instead he became a human being with fears and flaws. Don't you love him anymore, now that you know he's not perfect?"

"My love for Cas is not the questionable factor here. It's his love for me that is so undependable."

"Did he ever say he didn't love you anymore?"

"Not exactly."

"What exactly did he say?"

Lisel's mind scurried back in search of the exact words. "When we first got back to Chicago, he said that we should do some serious thinking about our relationship and that we shouldn't see each other in the interim."

"Did the subject of seeing other people ever arise?"

"No."

"Did he say when you'd resume seeing each other?"

"He said he'd call me."

"And did he?"

"I don't know. He claims he did, that I was out when he called."

"Do you think he's telling the truth?"

"I don't know what to think. That's the problem." Lisel

122

wearily shoved her plate aside, despite the fact that it was still half-full. "All I do know is that I don't want to get hurt again."

"How persistent do you think Cas will be?"

"Not very." Lisel shrugged. "I mean if he were serious about me, then he would've kept me as Hinkler's interpreter. That way he could've seen me every day."

"Maybe the bank has rules about getting involved with clients."

"I wouldn't have been his client. I just don't understand it, Kim. In Austria, Cas was so different. Here—I don't know what he's like."

"Then maybe we should find out."

"How?"

"A friend of mine works for the First American. He's a loan counselor there. I'll ask him if he's heard of Cas. Maybe he can shed some light on Cas's Chicago persona."

"I suppose it's worth a try," Lisel agreed.

A frustrating afternoon spent clearing up a backlog of paper work had Lisel ready to order a pizza by the time she let herself into her apartment. A quick phone call to the neighborhood pizzeria and a long shower helped restore her spirit. She was wrapped in a white terry-cloth robe, her wet hair engulfed in a matching white bath towel when she heard the rap of knuckles on her front door.

"Who is it?" she cautiously called through the wooden portal.

"Parlotti's Pizza!" a cheerful voice replied.

"Just a sec." She had to undo an intricate series of locks before she could open the door. When she did so, it was to exclaim, "You!"

CHAPTER EIGHT

"What are you doing here?" Lisel demanded.

"Delivering your pizza," Cas calmly replied. "Aren't you going to invite me in?"

"Taking on part-time work now, are you?" she asked mockingly.

"Consider this a special delivery." His gaze was all-encompassing and very masculine in its visual appreciation as he murmured, "I like your outfit."

Her robe wasn't meant for public display, and the hallway was becoming increasingly busy. In view of that fact, she said, "You'd better come in."

"This is a nice place you've . . . got." His compliment trailed off as his eyes scanned the room in disbelief.

Chrome and black leather furniture were spotlighted by track lighting. One entire wall was taken up with an awesome array of advanced stereo equipment. Artfully decadent Picasso etchings graced another wall while an alpaca rug lay at the altar of a free standing fireplace. The overall effect was unquestionably very expensive and, more important, very masculine!

"You live here?" Cas questioned in disbelief.

Lisel was beginning to enjoy herself. "Yes."

"Alone?"

"No." She watched his expression darken before relenting and adding, "I share it with a piranha."

"What's his name?" Cas growled.

"Edgar. He's over there in the tank."

"Tank?"

"That's where fish usually hang out. Even piranhas."

For the first time Cas noticed the large aquarium in the far corner. "You own a piranha?"

"Actually Edgar belongs to my cousin Hans. As does the apartment."

"Ah." His face wore a satisfied expression. "That explains the masculine decor."

"That's a sexist thing to say."

"Blame it on my empty stomach. I didn't have any lunch. Our pizza's getting cold, so let's eat."

"Wait a minute!" In an effort to deter him, she put a restraining hand on his arm.

It had no effect. Cas simply towed her along with him as he purposefully headed for the dining-room table.

Letting go of his arm, she irritatedly demanded, "Who said anything about your eating here?"

"I just did." He turned to shoot her an irresistible grin. "Didn't you hear me?"

"I thought my ears must be deceiving me," she marveled. "I couldn't believe you would have the nerve to invite yourself to dinner."

"Believe it. Where are your plates?"

Lisel stubbornly remained silent.

"Never mind, we don't need plates. We'll just stretch out in front of the fire—"

"What fire?"

Cas found the switch that activated the fireplace's gas

jet flames. "This one. Unless you'd rather we start a little kindling of our own?" Like the lick of fire, his eyes slid over her face and down her body, paying special attention to the expanse of her bare legs.

She protectively tightened the belt on her robe. "I'm going to go change."

"No, don't do that."

"Why not?" she belligerently demanded.

His reason was commendably practical. "Your pizza will get cold. Come on, sit."

"Where?"

"On the rug."

Lisel vetoed that idea. "I think we should eat at the table."

"But this is much cozier."

"I know. That's why we'll eat at the table. I'll get the plates."

Her escape to the kitchen was thwarted by his pursuit. "Need any help?"

"You can get the drinks out of the refrigerator."

"What does this cousin of yours do for a living anyhow?" Cas asked, tugging the refrigerator door open.

"He's a disc jockey for an FM rock station," she nonchalantly imparted.

"Mayer the Mouth!" Cas was flabbergasted. "Are you telling me your cousin is Mayer the Mouth?"

"That's not his christened name, no. But I believe that's what his listeners call him."

"Why are you living in his apartment?"

"I'm subletting it from him while he's doing penance in Europe for a few months."

"That's right." Cas returned his attention to the contents of the refrigerator. "I remember hearing about some trouble he had with the station management."

126

"Hans named the piranha after the station manager. They're not exactly the best of friends."

"Who? Hans and the station manager or the station manager and the piranha?"

"All of the above."

"What do you feed your piranha?"

"Uninvited dinner guests."

Cas laughed appreciatively. "I don't imagine you get many of those, not with Arnie downstairs to protect you. Your piranha must be pretty hungry by now. I know the feeling."

How did he manage to deflect all her comments? And how did he manage to stir her senses in spite of her better judgment?

Before these and other earth-shattering questions could be answered, Cas was posing a question of his own. "Why is there a padlock on your refrigerator's vegetable bin? Are you afraid someone is going to run off with your celery?"

"Hans keeps his important papers in there. He claims it's fireproof."

"So's a safety-deposit box." Cas selected two bottles of imported beer and shut the door.

"Hans doesn't trust banks." For good measure, she added, "And I don't trust bankers."

"Good thing I'm not a banker then."

His grin was too appealing for safety's sake. "You're an economist working in a bank." She hauled the plates down from their shelf. "In my book, that makes you a banker."

Cas followed her back to the dining room. "I'd like to read it sometime."

She looked at him in confusion. "What?"

"Your book." He stroked his index finger down her arm. "I'd like to write on your blank pages."

She removed her arm from his dangerous influence. "I don't have any blank pages."

"Does your book have a happy ending?"

"I'm not at the end yet. I'm still trying to eat my pizza." What was meant to be a scathing rejoinder came across as an affectionate grumble.

"Allow me." He pulled out a chair with the continental flourish he'd teasingly displayed in Austria the morning after they'd made love. *Forget it,* her eyes flashed. *I'm not going to make a fool of myself twice, no matter how charming you may be.*

His cocked eyebrow acknowledged her visual message, accepting the challenge and responding to it with a silent message of his own.

"I can see your hackles rising," he said teasingly. "Calm down and eat your pizza." He handed her a slice.

"Don't tell me what to do," she replied rebelliously.

"All right." He sat across from her "Then I'll eat your slice." He took her hand in his and guided the laden triangle to his mouth, biting into its thick crust. "*Mmm!* Delicious."

Lisel hastily retrieved her hand and her pizza. She tried hiding her discomposure beneath an instructional tone. "Chicago and pizza go way back, you know. The first—"

"Lisel, you're not my guide tonight." He kindly interrupted her to voice his assurance, "From here on out, I know my own way around."

His certainty angered her. "Is that why you dismissed me as Hinkler's interpreter? Did I make you feel threatened?"

Cas was unimpressed with her anger, treating it with good-natured humor. "The only time you made me feel threatened was when you stared daggers into me."

Lisel was not amused. "I would hardly call that grounds for dismissing me."

He swallowed a healthy bite of pizza and took a swig

128

of beer before saying, "They weren't grounds, and you weren't dismissed."

"We're back to semantics again, are we? First you didn't dump me, and now you didn't dismiss me."

"We have in-house translators to deal with clients. Your services simply weren't needed."

"Reuben told me that those in-house translators are not always used."

"Who's Reuben?" Cas suspiciously questioned.

"My boss. And he wasn't exactly pleased to hear that I'd lost Hinkler's account." He wasn't exactly furious either, but that was neither here nor there.

"I'm sorry about that. Would you like me to call and explain things to him?"

"How can you explain things to him when you can't explain them to me?"

"I did explain them to you. You just don't understand."

"Are you calling me stupid?"

"No, I'm not calling you stupid."

She glared at him over her slice of pizza. "It sounded like it to me."

His voice was matter-of-fact as he told her, "You're not going to make me lose my temper by carrying on like this."

"Then stop making *me* lose *my* temper. You're very good at making me angry."

"I noticed that," he ruefully acknowledged. "Not exactly the response I'm looking for, but better than indifference."

Lisel could never be indifferent to Cas, although she had no intention of telling him so. From the first moment she'd seen him, she'd been attracted to him, and with each increasing day that attraction had grown. She hadn't really fought it. Oh, she'd put up a mild protest about not wanting to get involved, but she hadn't launched any major battles, or even any minor ones, until they'd returned to Chicago.

Now Lisel was actively fighting her attraction to Cas, although it was difficult to do so when he was being so charming. *But for how long?* an inner voice warned. *How long until things get too serious and he calls it off again?*

"What are you frowning about?" the object of her thoughts inquired.

"You."

"You don't trust me anymore, do you?" He stated the words flatly, the impact of what he was saying clearly etching his expression. His features were drawn, his eyes dark with remorse.

Lisel was reluctant to increase his pain. "I don't know. Maybe it's more the way you feel that I don't trust," she analyzed.

His look of tight emotion eased as he murmured, "I can understand that. Since it took me a week to trust the way I feel about you, I guess I should give you some time, too. But, Lisel, I do know that what we shared together in Austria was something very special, a love worth fighting for. And I will fight for you. I have no intention of giving up."

"Maybe you just see me as some kind of challenge for you," she gently suggested. "When I loved you, there was no thrill of the chase. I wasn't running. Now that I am, you're interested again."

"I never stopped being interested in you," Cas corrected. "Never stopped being attracted to you, never stopped wanting or needing you."

The intensity of his gaze was penetrating her defenses. Rallying her wayward emotions, she voiced a cool reply. "Well, you'd better learn to stop because there's no future in it."

"I hurt you badly, I know that. And it cuts me up inside

130

to think what I've done to you. But, honey, I will make it up to you." His voice offered a soothing balm to her wounds.

"There's no need . . ." she began, only to be interrupted by his contradicting growl.

"Yes, there is. An aching, empty need that only you can fulfill."

Lisel fiddled with the edge of her robe, unaccustomed to Cas's harsh sincerity. Teasing charm and mocking flirtatiousness were more in her line of experience. The ragged desperation in his voice increased her uncertainty about her own feelings. She didn't want to love Cas. Did she? She shook her head with a sigh. How did life get so complicated?

The flickering firelight played over her changing expressions. Cas watched confusion, irritation, and self-doubt chase their way across her face.

"A schilling for your thoughts," he offered in a gentle voice.

She invented a white lie. "I was thinking I should get dressed."

"You've had a tough day. Why don't you go relax in front of the fire while I clear the table?" Cas was already efficiently gathering up the remains of their dinner.

You really should get dressed, she told herself. *Later,* she decided, succumbing to the tempting coziness of the fireplace and the welcoming softness of the alpaca rug. Staring into the fire, conjuring up images in the dancing flames, she was startled when Cas joined her.

Kneeling beside her, he announced, "I've got something for you," and reached into his jacket pocket and drew out a small wrapped object.

She viewed it suspiciously. "What is it?"

"Open it and you'll find out."

She cautiously did so. A moment later she was holding

131

a glass sphere in her hand. Enclosed in its center was a miniature Alpine scene, complete with craggy mountain peaks and a tiny onion-domed church. A bed of snow-flakes rested on the bottom.

"I saw that in a store window," he told her, "and thought of you."

Lisel shook it, likening the eddying swirl of snowflakes to the swirling, contradicting needs and desires coursing through her. Did she love Cas? Did she want to love Cas? Did she have a choice? Did she know what she wanted?

"Do you like it?" he asked, uncertain whether her thoughtful frown was a result of his gift or her own thoughts.

"It's lovely," she said with soft sincerity. "Thank you."

He was only a few inches away from her, close enough to be a temptation without posing a threat. They were face-to-face, knees almost touching. Expressive looks were exchanged—his as potent as a caress, hers shadowed with wariness.

"My hair's still wet," she murmured with self-conscious awkwardness. "I should go dry it."

"No, stay where you are," he huskily instructed. "I'll dry it for you." Gently unwrapping the terry-cloth turban, Cas released her hair from its damp confinement. It fell past her shoulders, curving over the slope of her breast.

Lisel's breath caught in her throat as his hand reached out toward her, but he only lifted a swatch of hair and enfolded it in the towel. "This towel's too wet. We need a dry one," he decided. "You stay put." His hand briefly pressed down on her shoulder in a physical reiteration of his words. "I'll get one from the bathroom."

"But you don't know where the bathroom is," she protested.

"Honey, I don't need a guide, remember?"

The thought of Cas's reaction to the wanton hedonism

132

of the black marble bathroom made her smile and say, "All right. Suit yourself."

She wasn't disappointed. He returned a few minutes later, still shaking his head. "Your cousin's taste is something else. That shower curtain should be X-rated."

Lisel's reply was muffled by the soft towel he'd draped over her head. She felt the flexing of each powerful finger as he patiently rubbed her hair dry. Gradually she relaxed under the tender attention and simply enjoyed the unaccustomed pampering. It felt good to be taken care of for a change. A feeling of almost feline contentment rose within her, curling her toes and inciting a human purr.

Misinterpreting the muffled sound for one of protest, Cas smoothed her hair with a final stroke and a wry comment. "I'm not very good at this."

"Oh, I wouldn't say that." The words were out of her mouth before she'd given thought to possible repercussions.

The look in his eyes was more expressive than mere words could ever be. He approached her with slow determination. Lisel made no move to escape. It was as if they both were tied to opposite ends of an ever-shortening silken rope, a rope that would soon bind them together in its invisible cords.

Her mind became a slate wiped clean of conscious thought, operating purely on a sensual level. In that poignant moment of anticipation, all her senses became more keenly attuned. The sound of her own heartbeat, the feel of the fire's heat, the projected warmth radiating from Cas, the hungry taste of desire—all were heightened. Her lashes tumbled shut, shielding the lambent hunger in her eyes.

Their lips met, merging in an artful blend of advance and retreat, adjusting to shape and texture only to repeat the process all over again before parting. His tongue explored the inner softness of her mouth with an expert thoroughness she'd come to expect from him.

The seeking persuasion of his kiss was reflected in the caressive explorations of his hands as they lifted to bracket the graceful column of her throat. One hand slid down to her collarbone, where it registered her accelerated pulse. The other moved around to tangle itself in the golden mass of her hair. Fingers, splayed in the spangled silkiness, unobtrusively sought the nape of her neck in order to pull her deeper into his embrace.

Lisel provided no resistance, responding with a supple pliancy that had little to do with surrender. Their kiss continued uninterrupted as Cas captured the lapel of her robe between his thumb and index finger. Inch by inch it was then maneuvered off her shoulder. Her whimper of surprised pleasure was incorporated into their kiss, a mere exhalation of breath.

His arms enfolded her, gathering her in. His wrist was braced at the nape of her neck, providing support as he, oh, so slowly, lowered her to the welcoming thickness of the alpaca rug. In one fluid motion he came down over her, his leg settling between hers.

The provocative pressure made her hungrily aware of the intimate differences between them. Her lower body melted against his heat. The resultant mingling of softness and hardness lured her further into his web of desire.

Lisel's arms tightened around Cas's waist, her hands impatiently tugging his shirt from the restrictive waistband of his pants. Once that was accomplished, she was free to rediscover the muscular resilience of his warm flesh. Her fingers crept up the hollows of his spine in ever-increasing eddies of passion, exciting him to a feverish pitch.

Cas expeditiously parted the already loosened lapels of her robe, revealing her creamy voluptuousness. A trail of warm, whispered kisses led him from her mouth to the newly revealed territory, where his tongue traced patterns of delight across the slope of her full breasts. Muffled compliments were muttered against the smoothness of her perfume-scented bare skin. Each sensitive peak was treated to an exquisite display of sensual attention that had the tips throbbing with taut arousal.

Her need for him became a palpable thing, creating an actual physical ache. Only as the pain increased did Lisel realize that the continual ache originated not from any of her erogenous zones, but from the gumline of her lower jaw. Her tooth! Awareness returned with a vengeance, the pain becoming too persistent to be ignored. Lisel struggled to be free.

Cas groaned a protesting "No," tightening his grip.

She struggled all the harder. "Let me go!"

Her voice held an element of panic that he couldn't overlook. The tremors rippling through his limbs spoke of the supreme effort it cost him not to take her right there and then. When he spoke, his voice was harsh with hard-won control. "Honey, you'd better have a good excuse."

His words ignited her anger. Of all the insufferable nerve! She wasn't answerable to him; she wasn't answerable to any man. Scrambling to her feet, she rewrapped her robe around her. Chin stuck out at a pugnacious angle, fists clenched by her sides, she looked like a fighter prepared to do battle. "Listen, mister, this is my apartment."

"Your cousin's apartment." Cas calmly corrected her, returning to his former game plan of staunch amiability.

"And you've got no rights here," she continued without pause. "I think you'd better leave."

"Not until you tell me why you pulled away from me."

"I wasn't in the mood."

"I don't buy that."

Her shoulders lifted in an indifferent shrug. "That's your problem."

"No, my problem is much more acute than that," he raggedly muttered.

Lisel kept her own counsel, which was just as well since the memory of his taut frame rendered her speechless.

Seeing that he was getting nowhere, Cas tried taunting the truth out of her. "Were you trying to tease me?"

"No!"

"Trying to see how far you could push me?"

"No!"

"Then what?" he shouted.

She shouted right back. "I have a toothache!"

Cas had the audacity to laugh.

Lisel, who didn't recognize his laughter as an indication of relief, yelled, "It's not funny! I'm afraid of dentists. No, correct that." Her hand sliced out in a decisive gesture. "I'm more than just afraid—I'm petrified."

His expression was coaxingly rueful as he admitted, "So am I."

"You must be kidding!" she said derisively, certain that Cas was mocking her affliction and not appreciating it one bit.

"Why do you say that?"

She grappled for a droll way of stating her reason, but all she came up with was the unvarnished "Because you're a man."

"I see. And men aren't allowed to have fears. Is that right?"

"No, that's not what I meant." Her denial was genuine. "It's just that men generally tend to deny their fears." Rick had almost hit her for once suggesting he was afraid of cats merely because he cringed whenever a friendly feline came near him. "Are you really afraid of going to the dentist?"

Cas looked her straight in the eye and said, "Yes."

"Why?"

His eyes took on a twinkle of humor. "A foolish desire to avoid pain."

Lisel's challenging look requested a more detailed explanation.

"I had the misfortune to injure a tooth in a skiing accident when I was a freshman in college." He grimaced in remembered pain. "Suffice it to say that the dentist I was sent to had the manual dexterity of an elephant and was extremely parsimonious with the novocaine. What's your excuse?"

"A root canal when I was eleven. Sometimes I still have dreams about it."

He nodded understandingly. "Teeth have long memories. But if your tooth does hurt, you'll have to go to a dentist."

"I know. I keep putting it off."

"I've found a great dentist who specializes in traumatized patients. Why don't I give him a call and set up an appointment for you?" Since it wasn't meant to be a question, Cas didn't bother waiting for an answer before heading for the nearest phone.

"You can't call him now," she protested.

"Sure I can. Watch." He punched the touch-tone buttons.

"You've memorized his number?"

"It's 'DR. TOOTH.' If this phone didn't have letters on it, I'd have been in trouble." His murmured aside included a mocking gesture directed at the streamlined receiver, which looked like an inhabitant of the twenty-first century. "Your cousin's phone, no doubt?"

She nodded, her lips lifting in a half smile that was wiped off when Cas spoke into the phone.

"Dr. O'Hara? This is Cas Kalensky. I'm sorry to call

137

so late, but my fiancée has a bad toothache, and it's cramping our style."

Lisel stared at Cas as if he'd lost his mind. Either that
or she'd lost her hearing! He couldn't have said she was
his fiancée, could he? And "cramping our style!"

"Thanks. I knew I could count on you." Cas blithely
continued with his phone conversation. "Tomorrow?
What time?"

Lisel was vehemently shaking her head, but she soon
had to stop because it made her tooth throb.

Cas ignored her frowning signs of refusal. "Six will be
fine. See you then." He returned the phone to its sculp-
tured cradle and told her, "It's all set. You've got an
appointment tomorrow evening at six."

Having made this announcement, he now headed toward a nearby drink decanter. When he returned to her
side, he was carrying two glasses with a healthy shot of
whiskey in each. He offered one to her. "Here, drink this.
Dentist's orders," he added, forestalling her protest.

She took a sip, grimacing as the raw spirits burned their
way down her throat. Suitably fortified, she lodged her
complaint at his high-handed behavior.

Cas let her have her say. When she was done, he dispelled her resentment with a few words. "Honey, I love
you, and I'm concerned about your welfare. If you'd rather go to another dentist, then that's fine with me. But
you've got to get your toothache taken care of. The longer
you wait, the harder it will be."

He'd done it again. How could she stay angry in the face
of such a romantic motivation? As she often did when
unsettled, Lisel gravitated toward the panoramic window
and the city skyline on display.

"It's a beautiful view, isn't it?" His voice reached
around from behind her, enfolding her in its warmth.

Contentment stilled her own voice as she observed her special nightly ritual.

Unbeknownst to her, Cas also observed it, reading her lips in the window's reflection. "Who were you saying good night to?"

Caught in the act, Lisel spoke the truth. "I was talking to the John Hancock Building."

Cas did a proverbial double take. "Come again?"

"The John Hancock Building. The one with the two antennas on top."

"I know which building it is, but I've never met anyone who spoke to buildings before."

Lisel turned to confront him. "I've got a good reason for doing so."

"This one I've gotta hear!" he said mockingly while surreptitiously removing the half-empty glass from her hand.

"I'm not drunk, so stop looking at me that way. My father works for that company." She pointed toward the John Hancock's twin blinking aerial lights.

"My father works for an electronics firm, but I don't talk to TVs."

"You've never talked much about your family. I don't even know if you have any brothers or sisters."

"You should have asked me when you gave me the third degree the day I checked into your cousin's hotel. I would have told you."

"I did not give you any third degree," she protested, just as he knew she would. "I was merely filling in your registration form."

"Sure you were."

The combination of whiskey and his taunting grin took her mind off her pain. "Are you going to tell me if you have any brothers or sisters?" she demanded in irritated exasperation.

"I have a younger stepsister."

"Stepsister?"

He nodded. "My mother died when I was seven. My stepmom really raised me."

"I'm sorry."

"Sorry my stepmom had the job of raising me?"

"No, sorry your mother died when you were so young."

His grin faded. "It's strange, but I can't remember my real mother at all."

"What were you like as a kid?"

"A hell raiser."

"Did you plan on being a banker when you grew up?"

"Not exactly. I was going to join the merchant marines."

"What happened?"

"I get seasick."

Lisel remembered his grin long after she should have been asleep. She tried telling herself that it was the nagging pain of her toothache that was keeping her awake, or the worry over her approaching dental visit. But that didn't explain the romantic direction of her thoughts.

After she had switched on her bedside radio, the soothing strains of the "Pachelbel Canon" filled the room. Lisel lay back on the lonely expanse of her pillow and let the music wash over her. Of its own accord, her mind wandered into forbidden realms. She saw herself in a simple medieval gown, her long hair bound in a thick braid and tied up with a band of pure gold.

Cas, her knight in shining armor, stood before her. He had discarded his armor, leaving only the warm, bare-chested knight. Like the hero in the book on her bedstand, he was a tender and chivalrous knight, with a passionate hunger in his eyes.

In her private fantasy her knight kissed her, kissed her

with a gossamer lightness that became increasingly evocative. His mouth moved over hers, each stroke of his tongue a ravishing delight. Then, in the true manner of knights, he picked her up and carried her off to his bed.

The music stopped, calling a halt to Lisel's daydream. Coming back to reality, she viewed her twentieth-century surroundings with first a regretful and then an angry sigh. What was meant to be a soothing musical break had turned out to be an inciteful interlude. A victim of unfulfilled desires, Lisel impatiently switched off the radio and vindictively hoped Cas was tossing just as restlessly as she!

Her hopes were realized as, three blocks away and two stories higher, Cas punched his pillows with a vehemence normally seen only in heavyweight boxing matches. Disgusted by his inability to sleep, he lay on his back, one arm braced beneath his head. Images of the scene in Lisel's apartment kept replaying themselves in his mind. Once more he felt the supple softness of her body beneath his, smelled the haunting fragrance of her perfume, yearned for what he'd been denied.

Sensual conjecture provided him with the picture of them lying before the fireplace, Lisel eager and responsive. She smiled up at him, her eyes that unique blend of blue ice and green fire. Like a spell-casting witch, she flowed over him, making love to him with such a magical inventiveness that it brought a smile to his lips and kept it there throughout the night.

141

CHAPTER NINE

Freshly cut flowers greeted Lisel when she arrived for work the next morning. Cas had substituted a postcard for his message, addressing it "To a magical witch from her hopeful knight in shining armor." The picture on the postcard was Botticelli's famous masterpiece "The Birth of Venus."

Kim, unaware of the nature of the postcard or the message it contained, shook her head in disappointment. "No roses?"

Lisel jammed the postcard back into its protective envelope, blushing like a schoolgirl all the while. She'd seen that painting numerous times before, had even visited the real thing in Florence's Uffizi Gallery. It had always been a favorite of hers. How had Cas known that? There was nothing blush-worthy in the artistic subject matter of the painting, although the well-endowed Venus was wearing only a smile and a few flowers. It was his use of the knight in shining armor analogy that brought to mind her sexual fantasy from the night before and brought a resultant flush to her cheeks.

Much to Lisel's embarrassment, an additional flower was delivered every hour. These held no printed message. None was required, for the flower was a rose, which got progressively darker as the day wore on. From the pure white bud delivered at 10:00 A.M. to the dusky blossom at 4:00, the seven flowers covered the full gradation of hues.

"This from an economist?" Kim was impressed. "I've got to meet this guy!"

She got her chance sooner than expected. At five to five he walked into the Linguistics office.

"I'm Cas Kalensky here to take Lisel to her dentist's appointment."

"So you're the economist, huh?" Kim eyed him in disbelief.

His eyes lit up. "Lisel's told you about me?"

"Your name has come up. In fact, today it was mentioned at least once an hour."

"The flowers arrived?"

"Every hour like clockwork. I'll tell Lisel you're here."

"No. Let me surprise her."

"It's your life." Kim's delicate eyebrows rose with audacious humor. "Third office on the left."

Cas knocked on the closed door before entering.

"Come in." Lisel, assuming it to be the delivery of her five o'clock rose, didn't look up from the report she was completing. "Put it over there." She aimed her pen toward the vase containing the other flowers.

"I'd rather put it here," Cas murmured, leaning over the front of her desk to graze her parted lips with the deliciously soft petals of a single red rose. He followed up the floral caress with a visual courtship that touched every part of her face and rested on her mouth with dedicated concentration.

When he spoke, it was to question matter-of-factly, "How's the tooth?"

143

Lisel hastily gathered her scattered senses and repeated her greeting of last night. "What are you doing here?"

"Making another special delivery." He laid the rose on top of her report.

She steadfastly refused to attach any special significance to the rose's color. Nevertheless her voice was soft as she thanked him. "You needn't have bothered delivering it yourself."

"No bother. I was coming to take you to the dentist anyway."

"You don't have to escort me." Softness was exchanged for resentment. "I'll keep my appointment."

"It's not a matter of escorting." The quietness of his denial made it all the stronger. "I thought you might need the moral support."

Lisel looked at him in silent wonder. Surely this was too good to be true and too good to last, wasn't it?

Cas frowned over her silence before gruffly saying, "If you'd really rather go on your own, I'll understand."

"No, I wouldn't rather go alone. Thanks for the offer."

"I'd offer you a lot more, but you wouldn't accept," he cryptically replied.

The moment Lisel stepped into the dentist's office, she wrinkled her nose. "I'd forgotten how bad these places can smell."

Cas's face mirrored her aversion. "A unique blend of antiseptic and anesthetic."

He sat beside her as she filled out the informational form, watching her write and helpfully supplying half the answers for her. "Birth date, two three fifty-eight."

"I do know my own birthday," Lisel protested, but without any real vehemence. She appreciated his attempts to keep her mind off the impending appointment.

144

When she reached the special remarks section of the form, she wrote "EXTREME FEAR OF DENTISTS!"

"Dr. O'Hara will be with you in a few minutes," the receptionist informed her with a friendly smile.

Lisel reluctantly returned to her seat.

"Chin up," Cas coaxed.

"Thanks." Her laugh was shaky. "But if I do that, the dentist will drill a hole through my mouth."

"I wouldn't let any harm come to that mouth of yours; you should know that." His grin was positively lecherous and successfully sidetracked Lisel's attention, even if it was for a short amount of time.

When a uniformed hygienist approached her and asked, "Lisel?" for a crazy moment she was tempted to say, "No, never heard of her," and leave, but Cas's presence prevented that.

The examining area looked nothing like the cubbyhole arrangement she remembered from the last dentist she'd been to. The floor was carpeted; the room, filled with plants. A hanging mobile had Snoopy perennially chasing the Red Baron. An adult rock station provided background music.

"Hi, Lisel. I'm Kathy. There's nothing to be nervous about."

Easy for you to say.

The hygienist surprised her by staying with her, making pleasant conversation about the weather, Chicago politics, the latest cover of *Time* magazine. Her company helped keep the panic at bay, so that by the time the dentist arrived Lisel was beginning to relax.

"Hi, Lisel." Again the personal greeting. "I'm Dr. O'Hara. Relax, we're not going to hurt you."

Sure you're not.

"I understand one of your teeth is giving you trouble."

Lisel nodded. *Why else would I be here?*

145

"Which one?"

She pointed.

"Okay. Open wide. I'm just going to look, so you don't have to worry." He patted her shoulder reassuringly.

I've heard that before.

The X ray Dr. O'Hara decided on took only a few minutes to take and develop. Lisel was given a pair of headphones and the tape of her selection to listen to while she waited—a far cry from being abandoned in a sterile office.

Upon his return the dentist told her, "There's a cavity in your right lower molar. It's under another filling."

Great.

"Would you like some novocaine?"

"Do I have a choice?"

"Of course you do. You're the patient. It's your tooth; you're in charge. But judging from the depth of the cavity, I would recommend some kind of anesthetic. We can give you some nitrous oxide gas, if you prefer."

Gas? No way! "Novocaine is fine."

"Before I give you the shot, I'm going to coat your gum with cherry juice. It works as a natural anesthetic, so you won't feel the needle as much."

I've never heard of that one before.

"There, that wasn't so bad, was it?"

Lisel shook her head. Compared to the pain of her toothache, it hadn't been very bad.

"Okay, now we'll wait until that takes effect. But I want to assure you that when we start drilling, you have only to raise your right hand and I'll stop at any time. You'll be in charge of the pace, okay?"

Under this kind of assurance, Lisel felt the intensity of her fear lessening. She actually leaned back in the fully reclining dental chair and took an interest in her surroundings. Directly above her, tacked onto the ceiling,

146

was a poster saying, "You only live once—but if you do it right, once is enough." She found herself staring at that poster quite a bit during the next twenty minutes, while the dentist worked on her tooth.

"If you do it right, once is enough." The same could be said about love. Why was it so hard to do it right, to fall for the right man and have him return your love in the right way? She'd thought that Cas was the right man for her. Was she wrong to hold back when he was trying to make amends? All Lisel knew was that this time she had to be sure; she couldn't afford any more mistakes.

"The Chinese torture instrument, please," the dentist briskly requested.

Lisel's eyes rounded.

"Sorry." Dr. O'Hara patted her shoulder. "I didn't mean to scare you. That's just a nickname for this strange-looking clamp. All it really does is hold your tongue in place while I fill your tooth. It doesn't hurt."

It didn't, and in no time she was reentering the front reception area, proudly displaying the green shamrock Dr. O'Hara had awarded her for bravery.

"How was it?" Cas questioned her, as concerned as a prospective father.

"Not as bad as I expected," Lisel answered, her voice a little strange because of her still-numbed lower lip.

"Few things are." He touched the lapel of her dark wool blazer. "I see you were given a shamrock. You must have done well!"

"She did fine," the dentist assured Cas. Turning to Lisel, he advised, "No liquids or food until the numbness wears off." Grinning at Cas, he added, "No fooling around until then either!"

"I'd forgotten O'Hara's irrepressible sense of humor," Cas grumbled as they rode the elevator from the dentist's eighth-floor office.

"Why did you tell him I was your fiancée?"

"I don't think you're ready for the answer to that question yet."

"What makes you think I'll ever be ready?"

"My faith in the love we share."

"Cas," she halfheartedly protested.

He stroked the unaffected side of her face. "I'm proud of you. You came through the ordeal with flying colors."

His concern and tenderness chipped away at her defenses with more effectiveness than brute strength could ever achieve. And so it was that she made no protest when Cas insisted on coming up to her apartment and staying with her.

"Here, lie down on the couch." He led her over to said piece of furniture. As she made herself comfortable, so did he, removing his suit jacket and rolling up his shirt sleeves. "I'll see if there's anything good on the TV." Having picked up the program guide, he thumbed through it before exclaiming, "Bingo!"

Lisel threw him a quizzical look. "We're going to watch bingo?"

Cas shook his head.

"Then what?"

"You'll see." He turned the channel selector to a UHS station and then joined her on the couch. His "You're gonna like this" immediately made her suspicious. Even so, she couldn't believe her eyes when the names Clark Gable and Claudette Colbert flashed across the screen. It couldn't be! Could it? It was—right there written in black and white. *It Happened One Night.*

"Isn't there anything else on?" she inquired with mumbled casualness.

"Nope."

The movie brought back memories, memories she'd rather forget but couldn't resist harboring. Memories of a

148

certain night in the Alps when the walls of Jericho between herself and Cas had come crashing down for a resultant celebration of lovemaking that had been nothing short of sheer perfection. The night when her body had gained the most intimate knowledge of his, had known the supreme pleasure of loving satisfaction. Her flashbacks were becoming increasingly explicit, her sensual memory banks providing clamorous stimulation. This had to stop!

Her voice was slightly strangled as she inhospitably hinted, "Don't bankers have to get up early in the morning?"

"Tomorrow's Saturday."

So it was. "I'm surprised you don't have a hot date tonight."

"Who says I don't?"

Her expression froze. "Then don't let me detain you."

"You're not."

"Meeting her later, are you?" Icicles dripped from each syllable.

"No, I'm sitting next to her now."

The warmth of his gaze melted her iciness. Her knight in shining armor was apparently immune to frostbite. Actually it would be closer to the truth to say that he knew how to raise her temperature!

When the phone rang during a commercial, Cas said, "I'll get it." Before Lisel could protest, he had.

"It's Kim," he identified while handing over the receiver.

"Was that Cas?" Kim demanded, without bothering with a greeting.

"Yes," Lisel confirmed.

"What's he doing there?"

"Answering my phone."

"And what else?"

"Nothing."

149

"I get it. You can't talk, right?"

"Something like that," Lisel pleasantly agreed.

"Can we meet this weekend? I got a report back from my friend at the bank. I think you'll find it very interesting."

"Can't you tell me about it now?"

"With Cas standing in the same room with you? *Unh-unh.*"

"Okay. How about Sunday morning brunch?"

"Sounds great. That new place near you?"

"Right. The Market. I'll make the reservations. Eleven okay?"

"Fine. Meet you there."

By the time the movie was over the novocaine was beginning to wear off. Seeing the white tenseness of her face, Cas strode off to the bathroom and returned to hand her a glass and two tablets. "They're just aspirin-free pain relievers," he reassured her. "Dr. O'Hara said you might need them once the anesthetic wore off."

"Thank you." She swallowed the pills with the glass of water he handed her. "It's getting late." And now that she thought about it, she felt pretty rotten. "Shouldn't you be leaving soon?"

"I will. But first . . ." He got up and retrieved a small package from his jacket pocket.

"What's this?"

He held it up for her inspection. "What's it look like?"

"A present."

He flashed her a congratulatory grin. "Right."

"For me?"

"No, it's for Edgar," he mocked. "Of course it's for you. Open it."

Lisel found herself viewing Cas's enthusiasm with an element of possessive indulgence. He seemed to get as much fun out of giving her things as she did receiving

150

them. And she had to admit, it was fun receiving a
. . . "What is it?"

"Haven't you ever seen a Guatemalan worry box
before?"

"No, I can't say that I have."

"You have now. Look inside," he instructed.

"Is it safe?"

"You worry too much. That's why I got this for you."
He took the straw lid off the oval box and showed her the
handmade tiny people inside. "You see, every night you
tell your problems and worries to these worry people and
then let them worry about it for you."

Lisel was touched by his gift. "I don't know what to
say."

"Say you'll take it to bed with you and put it under your
pillow." She didn't need to see his face to know that he was
wearing his licentious grin again.

"Why, certainly I'll take it to bed with me. In fact, I
think I'll turn in right now. Since you don't need a guide,
I'm sure you can find your own way out, can't you?"

Cas ruefully acknowledged her words by picking up his
jacket and heading for the door. "I'll be back in the morning."

"The morning? Why?"

"Because I'm taking you out."

"Where?"

"It's a surprise. Dress casually." He was gone before she
could voice an objection.

"Now will you tell me where we're going?" Lisel asked
when Cas ushered her into his car the next morning.

"To meet a friend of mine." He shut the passenger door
for her.

She continued her questioning as soon as he slid behind
the wheel. "Male or female?"

151

"Male." The BMW came to purring life.

"What's his name?"

"Thor."

"Thor what?"

"I just call him Thor." Cas checked for a break in the traffic before pulling out and heading toward the lake.

"Why are you taking me to meet him?"

"Because it's a beautiful day and I love you."

What could she say to that?

"Relax." He smiled. "Just sit back and enjoy the music."

Lisel paid scant attention to Simon and Garfunkel's tongue-in-cheek song "At the Zoo." "You sound like Dr. O'Hara. Are we going to the park?" she asked, noting their proximity to Lincoln Park.

"Close."

She read the sign on the parking lot. "The zoo?"

"Bingo!"

"We're meeting your friend at the zoo?"

He fitted the BMW alongside a Chevette. "Anything wrong with that?"

"Not at all. Lead on."

Cas led her through the zoo grounds, not stopping until they reached the polar bears. "Well, what do you think of him?"

"Who?"

"Thor."

She looked at the surrounding crowd. "Where is he?"

"In there." Cas pointed over the fence.

"But there are only bears in there."

"That's right. Thor's the one on the left."

Lisel couldn't believe what she was hearing. "Your friend Thor is a polar bear?"

Cas nodded. "Isn't he impressive?"

"How can you be friends with a polar bear?"

152

"I'm one of his sponsors."

"Sponsors? For what?" she asked. "College? The Olympics?"

"I've adopted him."

"Thor's a little big for adoption, don't you think?"

"He is big, isn't he?" Cas proudly noted. "Did you know that newborn polar bear cubs weigh only about fifteen pounds, yet by the time they're fully grown they can weigh well over a thousand?"

"That's amazing." But she was looking at Cas, not at Thor. What kind of man gave a girl worry boxes and adopted a polar bear? The kind of man she'd fallen in love with. This was the Cas she'd known and loved in Austria. Spontaneous, fun-loving, romantic.

They spent the entire day at the zoo, visiting all the areas, including the world-famous ape house. While strolling hand in hand through the Farm-in-the-Zoo, they bestowed personalized names on the animals, like Persnickety the Pig, Crabby the Chicken, and Bumptious the Bull.

Lisel's buoyant mood led to her acceptance of Cas's dinner invitation. If their day had been youthfully exuberant, their evening was traditionally romantic. He took her out for dinner at one of the city's most expensive restaurants, complete with champagne, the works. Afterward they went dancing in a rooftop lounge, where the stars sparkled down at them through glass skylights.

By the time her head hit the pillow that night Lisel was well on her way to falling in love with Cas Kalensky all over again. And she found that prospect quite frankly terrifying.

Which was the real Cas—the one who wore blue jeans and bought her balloons at the zoo or the one who wore tailored suits and drove a BMW? Maybe Kim would be able to help answer that question tomorrow.

153

CHAPTER TEN

"This is some kind of feast." Kim marveled, eyeing the heavily laden dessert table they had to pass on their way to their seats. "How come you always know the best places to eat?"

"As a chocoholic, I make it my business to know these things," Lisel teasingly replied. "Some of the best chocolate desserts in the city are over there on that table."

"I'm glad to see that going to the dentist on Friday didn't deaden your sweet tooth." At Lisel's intentional grimace, Kim grinned and added, "No pun intended."

"I just read a study that claimed there's something in chocolate that's very good for reducing stress."

"Stress caused by Cas Kalensky, no doubt."

Now that Kim had brought up the subject, Lisel said, "I can't stand the suspense. Tell me what your friend said about Cas."

"My contact doesn't claim to be a close friend of Cas's," Kim warned. "Just a working associate."

Lisel's nod acknowledged the difference. "And?"

"And it appears that your economist leads a very calm,

154

very regulated existence here in Chicago. He's described as conscientious and hardworking, exceptionally intelligent, but not the kind of guy who'd paint the town red, or any other color for that matter."

Lisel found that hard to believe. The description sounded like an economist to be sure, but not her knight in shining armor. "You've met Cas. What do you think?"

"I think you've gotten hold of a closet romantic."

"I suppose it's possible that Cas has gotten locked into this traditional banker image here in Chicago," Lisel mused, "an image he broke when he went on vacation because he was certainly romantic in Austria!"

"I wouldn't say he's been doing that badly here in Chicago either," Kim stated with teasing approval. "Flowers every hour! That shows quite a sentimental flair."

"Yes, it does, doesn't it?" Lisel's smile was decidedly satisfied.

"You're smirking again," Kim said reproachfully. "Do you think we could continue this conversation after I've filled my plate? I'm starving, and the line at the buffet is getting longer by the minute."

Kim started at one decoratively arrayed table; Lisel, at another. That was because Lisel had her own way of approaching buffets, a sort of chronological order. First came the breakfast types of dishes, then salads and warm luncheon selections. Since Kim preferred the spontaneous sampling method, it was inevitable that they would get separated while serving themselves.

Lisel was debating over a selection of fresh baked rolls when she got the distinct feeling that someone was watching her. Looking up, she found herself staring into Cas's face.

"What are you doing here?"

155

"You really are going to have to come up with another salutation," he chastised her. "That one's getting trite."

Lisel bristled at having her greeting called trite. "What would you suggest I say? 'Fancy bumping into you here'?"

" 'I love you' would be nice. Or 'It's great to see you.' As to what I'm doing here, I'm eating brunch. Or about to." He indicated the empty plate in his hand. "What would you recommend?"

She eyed his innocent expression with exasperation. "That you give this up."

"Okay, I'll skip the rolls. What about the scrambled eggs?"

As they moved on to each new culinary offering, Cas asked for her opinion. Whenever Lisel reached for a serving spoon, he contrived to have his hand on it. His sotto voce comments, like "We have to stop meeting like this," made it difficult for her to maintain her distance.

"Are you here alone?" she broke down to ask.

"No, I'm here with friends."

"I didn't know they let polar bears in this restaurant," she mocked.

"Hey!" Cas immediately jumped to Thor's defense. "I think my polar bear is a lot better than the jerboa you adopted."

"It was between that and an American tarantula." While at the zoo Lisel had signed up for the fund-raising A.D.O.P.T. program, but her choice of animal had been limited by her budget. "Besides, jerboas are kind of cute."

"Cute?" He raised his brows in disbelief. "Thor is cute."

"Nothing that weighs a thousand pounds qualifies as being cute."

"Well, your jerboa is nothing more than a rodent."

"Rodents are mammals." She heatedly defended her adoptee. "Just like polar bears."

"Oh, yeah?"

"Yeah."

Their good-natured arguing ended in laughter.

"I hope your visit to the dentist hasn't put you off chocolate," Cas murmured with a significant glance at the dessert table.

"Afraid not." She added a dollop of sour cream to her cheese blintz, filling her plate with the last of her breakfast items. The only drawback to following this chronological method was that desserts were last. She cast her own envious glance at the selection of chocolate goodies. "I'm hooked for life."

"So am I. Hooked on you." The sensual promise of Cas's voice was even more appetizing than the chocolate.

Their eyes met and clung as they stared at each other over a warming dish full of blintzes. The sound of impatient complaining made them realize they were holding up the line and brought them back to earth.

Lisel's face reflected momentary confusion as Cas returned the serving spoon to the sour cream and hurriedly guided them both out of the main flow of traffic.

She said, "I'd better get back to Kim."

"Yes, and I'd better get back to my friends," Cas said reluctantly. His fingers lingered on the mauve silkiness of her long-sleeved blouse, transforming the courteous guidance of a moment ago into the intimacy of a caress. "Have dinner with me on Wednesday?" His fingers continued sliding down the length of her arm until they came to rest at her wrist, where they sensitively traced her pulse. "I could fix us something special at my place."

"I'm sure you could," she archly murmured.

"Would it make you feel better if I invited another couple as well?"

Perhaps meeting his friends would help her get a fix on Cas. So far she'd met only Thor, and the polar bear hadn't provided much information.

157

"Yes," she answered.

"Yes, it would make you feel better or you, you'll come?"

"Yes to both of the above."

"Great! If I weren't working late Monday and Tuesday, I'd invite you sooner."

"That's all right. A day or two doesn't make that much difference."

"Oh, yes, it does." Determination flashed across his face. "And someday soon you're going to acknowledge that fact."

Lisel was still standing there, staring after his retreating form, when Kim's voice reached her. "What happened to you? I thought you fell in."

"I ran into Cas."

Kim looked around in surprise. "Cas is here?"

Lisel nodded.

"How romantic. He must be following you."

"He lives only a few blocks from here," Lisel felt obligated to point out.

"I still say he's a closet romantic."

By Tuesday afternoon Lisel was forced to agree with her. She'd been inundated with gifts, small tokens that tied into the time they'd spent together. One such gift was a stuffed polar bear accompanied by a cute toy mouse; "the closest I could come to a jerboa," Cas noted on the attached tag. In deference to her love for chocolate, Cas had sent her a lavish box of Godiva chocolates along with a certified chocoholic pin.

"Cas," Lisel had protested Monday night when he'd phoned her during his twenty-minute dinner break, "you have to stop sending me things."

"Must I?" He sighed dramatically.

"The delivery charge alone on these things is going to be exorbitant."

"If you insist, I'll economize."

And so he did, by dropping off his present with Arnie. "This is one of my favorite answers to those 'What's black and white?' riddles," Cas had written on an accompanying note. "I have a feeling it may be a passion we share, one of many passions we'll share!" Inside the package was a box of Oreo cookies.

"Hey, this guy's too good to be true," Kim exclaimed when another batch of red roses arrived at the office, this time arranged in an Austrian crystal vase.

"I know." Lisel sighed, fingering the soft petals. "I worry about that."

"I was only kidding, but you sound serious."

"I am serious. Sometimes I think things seem too perfect, that something will happen to ruin it."

"I wouldn't worry about perfection," Kim heartily assured. "After all, you're not perfect, and neither is Cas. He does have flaws."

"Flaws?" Lisel bristled. Criticizing Cas was a right exclusively reserved for herself!

"Sure. He's afraid of dentists."

"So am I," Lisel quickly retorted.

"There. You see?" Kim declared triumphantly. "The perfect couple!"

Wednesday night was slow to arrive. Even though she'd spoken to Cas a few times on the phone, she'd missed seeing him. Wanting to make a good impression on his friends, she'd taken special care in dressing for the occasion. The end result was a look that was both appealing and approachable. Her customary smart suit had been replaced by a crepe dress. Her hair had been left loose, and her makeup was a medley of this fall's subtle colors.

All in all she felt pretty good about herself as she stood in the foyer of Cas's building, a former warehouse that had

159

been imaginatively converted into high-demand condominiums. She pressed the buzzer beneath his name and heard his voice come over the speaker. "Stay there a minute. I'll be right down."

"What happened?" she asked when, true to his word, he appeared in the foyer a minute later. "I thought we were eating at your place. Did you burn the dinner?"

"No, I did not burn the dinner, although *I'm* definitely feeling a little charred around the edges myself." The blaze of passion that flared in his eyes lent credence to his words.

"You don't look charred." Lisel managed to tease him, although her voice was somewhat on the unsteady side. In truth he looked fabulous! Casual but well dressed in a black velvet jacket, a cream silk shirt, and charcoal pants.

Unaware of her thoughts, Cas guided her through the glass double doors to the elevator, which opened horizontally instead of vertically. "Some people have trouble with the elevator"—he belatedly answered her original question—"so I thought I'd come give you a hand with it." When he tugged down on the canvas handle, the doors slid shut like a giant metal jaw.

"How's your tooth?" he asked as the former freight elevator lumbrously progressed upward.

"All better." They were talking like polite strangers.

"No pain?"

"None."

"Good. Because I don't think I can last another second without this." All pretense of social courtesy disappeared as Cas snared her in his arms, his lips claiming hers.

Lisel's response to the kiss was immediate and reflected an equal hunger. She'd gone too long without him, and her self-inflicted abstinence was beginning to tell. Her left arm completely encircled his neck, her fingertips brushing through his hair before grasping his shoulder to pull herself closer.

Even after the elevator had arrived at its destination and come to a ponderous halt, Cas still prolonged the kiss, his mouth seducing hers until the jawlike elevator doors were yanked open by an impatient tenant.

"I haven't been caught necking in a public place since I was a teen-ager," Cas ruefully stated as he led her to his door a few moments later.

"I think you shocked your neighbor," Lisel told him, remembering the look on the elderly man's face when he'd realized what he'd interrupted.

"No doubt about it. In fact, you'd better come inside before I'm kicked out of the building for such reprehensible behavior," he teased.

She looked around her with interest. The high-ceilinged living room reflected his eclectic tastes. A modern conversation pit coexisted in peaceful harmony with an antique rolltop desk. An abstract painting picked up the predominantly red colors of the Oriental rug. Like a blending of his favorite songs, "Jailhouse Rock" and the "Pachelbel Canon," the room reflected the best of many periods.

Considering that she'd just thought of the canon, it was almost spooky to identify its haunting melody coming through his speaker system. "It's a new digital recording I got for you," he explained with a grin.

"Cas, I feel bad accepting all these gifts from you."

"You don't like them?" He looked surprisingly hurt.

"Of course I like them," she hastily reassured him.

"Then there's no more to be said about it."

One look at his face told her protest would be useless, so she changed the subject. "Tell me something about your friends."

"I feel it only fair to warn you that Christopher and

161

Karyn are so happily married they may tempt you to take the plunge."

"Are you warning me not to get matrimonial ideas?" she countered.

"Quite the opposite." His loving finger tapped the tip of her nose. "I'm hoping you will get ideas. I know you're the one woman I love, the one I want. Someday soon I hope you'll know that, too."

"You make it all sound so easy." She sighed.

"It is easy. Resisting is what's hard."

"I've managed to resist this far."

"I know you have." His voice deepened, reflecting varying shades of intimate intent. "But I also know your resistance is lowering. I can see it in your eyes."

"Does that mean you can stop the chase?" she felt impelled to demand.

"Not at all. It gives me the inspiration to continue."

The arrival of Cas's friends precluded a reply on her part. After the introductions had been made, Karyn was the first to speak. "It's good to meet you." The smiling redhead immediately put Lisel at ease.

"My wife's been dying of curiosity," Christopher imparted with husbandly indulgence.

Christopher Reid was tall and handsome, with a ready smile. His wife obviously adored him, but that didn't stop her from jabbing him in the ribs with her elbow for what she called "divulging family secrets."

The dinner was a success, from both the culinary and the conversational point of view. Cas indeed had not burned the steaks, or anything else for that matter. During the meal the discussion naturally turned to travel with everyone promoting favorite locations.

"Bermuda!" Christopher and Karyn agreed with each other but not with Lisel and Cas, who replied, "The Alps!"

"The mountains are too cold." Karyn shivered. "I prefer the warmth of the sandy beach and the peacefulness of the azure ocean."

"You're starting to sound like a travel brochure," her husband teasingly warned.

"I can't help it. Bermuda holds special memories for me."

"We spent our honeymoon there," Christopher explained. They'd also been reunited there, but that was another story!

After dinner Christopher demanded to see the new computer investment program Cas had been bragging about. The two men took off for Cas's study, leaving the two women alone.

Karyn spoke first. "I understand Cas took you to the Lincoln Park Zoo."

Lisel nodded. She was beginning to wonder how much the Reids knew about her relationship with Cas.

"You should feel honored. Cas doesn't take many people to meet Thor."

Lisel's answering smile lacked the naturalness previously reflected.

"Relax," Karyn teased. "I'm not going to start lecturing you about what a terrific guy Cas is."

"You're not?"

Karyn shook her head. "All I'll tell you is that he's been a great friend to us."

"How did you meet?"

"Christopher applied for a loan."

"And Cas gave it to him," Lisel filled in.

"No, Cas turned him down." Lisel's baffled look made Karyn laugh. "I admit it was an inauspicious beginning for a friendship, but Cas's department had a programming project coming up, and he recommended Christopher's firm for the job. The project precluded the need for the loan. Cas was right; our problem was only a matter of short-term cash flow, although it felt worse than that at the time. Now I have only one question to ask you."

Here it comes. Lisel braced herself for an interrogation into her feelings for Cas.

Instead Karyn asked, "Does your bathroom shower curtain really have a picture of a—"

"Yes," Lisel hastily interrupted. "But it's not actually my shower curtain. It's my cousin's."

"I know. Mayer the Mouth. Oh!" Karyn clapped a hand over her own mouth. "I probably shouldn't call him that, I'm sorry."

"Don't be. I'm getting used to hearing him called that. In fact, I'm afraid that the next time I see him, I might refer to him that way myself!"

"Are you expecting him back soon?"

"The last I heard, he was due back sometime after Christmas," Lisel answered.

"Well, did you two talk about us when we were gone?" Cas demanded as he and Christopher reentered the room.

"Very little," Karyn teased. "Sorry."

"I like your friends," Lisel said after Christopher and Karyn had made their departure an hour later.

"And they liked you." Noticing her seeming absorption with his oversize windows, he asked, "Do you like my view?"

"You know I do. Why didn't you tell me that you have the same view I do?"

"I was saving that as my trump card. If all else failed, I planned on hiring the Goodyear blimp to hover over the John Hancock Building with 'CAS LOVES LISEL' illuminated on the side."

She turned away from the view. "You wouldn't!"

Cas didn't bother with a verbal reply. Instead he slipped his arms around her and nuzzled the sensitive skin beneath her ear. But when he would have gathered her closer, Lisel pulled away.

"Now what's the matter?" he ruefully demanded.

"We need to talk. There's something still bothering me."

"What?"

"Your reasons for dismissing me as Hinkler's interpreter."

He made an impatient gesture with his hand. "How many times do I have to tell you that I didn't dismiss you?"

"Whatever you call it, there's more here than meets the eye."

His eyes avoided hers. "You're making mountains out of molehills."

"Ah, but you forget, I've had a lot of experience with mountains. I know one when I see it."

"It had nothing to do with you" was his impatient dismissal.

She immediately jumped at that, demanding, "Then what did it have to do with?"

"Hinkler," he reluctantly admitted.

Lisel's eyes narrowed in concentration. The pieces were beginning to fall into place. Hadn't Reuben told her that Hinkler had a questionable business reputation?

"Tell me about your work," she invited, dropping onto his couch and patting the seat invitingly.

"My work!" Cas viewed her change of subject with marked suspicion.

"That's right." She casually leaned back to ask, "Do you always get assigned the troublesome cases?"

One look at his astonished face was answer enough. As he would've said, Bingo! "That's it, isn't it?" she exclaimed with excitement. "You get assigned the fishy cases

165

and didn't want me hanging around a character like Hinkler."

"Wait a minute here. I never said that."

"You didn't have to. I saw the look on your face."

Cas toyed with a denial before eventually discarding the idea. "How come I can be diplomatically evasive with everyone except you?"

"We've always been direct with each other," she softly replied. "Sometimes painfully so."

"I can't deny that."

"And you won't deny getting assigned the fishy cases?"

"I'm an economist, not a fisherman."

"Don't try to shoot me down with semantics. You know what I'm talking about. But I can understand your reluctance to talk about it. This is probably confidential, right?"

Cas didn't voice a reply, but his glance was intended to inhibit further discussion.

It didn't work. Having solved the first mystery so successfully, Lisel felt she was on a winning streak. "There's still one thing I don't understand, though. You must have heard about Hinkler's shady past."

"I've been informed of it, yes."

"Then what's the problem? Why even let Hinkler come into your bank in the first place?"

Cas sighed, running a weary hand around the back of his neck. "Mere innuendo isn't a sufficient reason for me to refuse a loan request." He shoved his hands into his pants pocket and began striding around the room. "Besides, granting the loan would lead to the opening of a manufacturing plant in a depressed area of the city. That would create jobs and lower the unemployment rate. Chicago is naturally interested in creating a good environment for business investments to be made here. Especially since several other cities are also vying for this particular project."

"Is Hinkler still in Chicago?"

"No, he's gone on to Phoenix to speak to a bank there. He'll be back in Chicago in a couple of days."

A couple of days. That would give Lisel a chance to do a little research of her own.

Pleased with her new receptiveness, Cas didn't question the determined glint he observed in her eyes. Instead he involved her in a romantic initiation of his conversation pit. Although vividly responsive, Lisel stopped short of going to bed with him. With success so near at hand. Cas reluctantly agreed to give her a little more time. But when he phoned her at work the next afternoon, he was no longer sure he'd made the right decision.

"I'm sorry, Cas," Kim informed him, "but Lisel isn't in. She's out of the office." And, as far as Kim was concerned, out of her mind to have agreed to go out with the Pincher, Fritz Schultz, even if it was only for drinks. Lisel claimed to have her reasons, all of which somehow revolved around Cas. That's all she'd been willing to tell Kim before swearing her to secrecy.

"When do you expect her back?" Cas demanded. Something was decidedly fishy here. The terminology brought to mind Lisel's use of the same word last night. Damn it, he should never have let her go.

"I believe she's left for the day."

Cas glanced down at his watch. It was only four. "Why did she leave? Is she ill?"

"No."

"Then what prompted her early departure?"

"I really can't say, Cas." That much was true anyway, Kim thought to herself. "I'm sorry, but I've got another call coming in, and I have to go. Good-bye, Cas."

Cas tried calling Lisel at home, but there was no answer. Deciding he could get more information in person, he took

167

off early and stopped by Linguistics' office to confront Kim.

"What's going on out here?" Reuben indignantly demanded, having heard Cas's impatient voice all the way through his closed door.

"I'm looking for Lisel Mayer," Cas stated, undeterred by the smaller man's obvious state of agitation.

"She's with a client," Reuben answered.

"I thought you said she'd left for the day." Cas turned to accuse Kim.

"She has," Kim maintained.

"With this client?" His gaze dared her to lie.

Kim reluctantly nodded.

Cas was waiting for Lisel when she finally arrived at her apartment building precisely two hours and fifty-one minutes later. "Where have you been?" he angrily growled, commandeering her elbow and propelling her into the elevator.

Lisel had a present to give him, and she didn't want to mar its presentation with misunderstandings. "Where I was isn't important," she hurriedly dismissed.

"It is to me. Were you alone?"

Unwilling to lie, she said, "No."

"Were you with a man?"

"Yes, but, Cas, wait until you hear—"

"Who was it?"

Intent on finding her keys and unlocking her door, Lisel didn't follow the line of questioning. "Who was who?"

"This man you were out with."

"A client." She unlocked the first two locks. "His name isn't important. It's what I found out that's important." The last lock was undone. "Come on," she coaxed, stepping inside. "Stop standing there glaring at me. I've got good news." She kicked off her shoes and dropped her purse on the couch.

Following her progress with his eyes, he delivered a warning. "It had better be real good!"

"It is. The key to your mystery."

Cas transferred his attention from her legs to her words. "What mystery?"

"About Hinkler."

"I think you'd better begin at the beginning," he strongly suggested.

"That's what I'm trying to do." She settled into a black leather chair before continuing her narrative. "After going over the Hinkler case with you," she said in her best detective manner, "I decided to check tactfully with some of the prominent German business contacts I have. That's why I went out tonight with Fritz. I thought I'd pump him for information about Hinkler." When Cas made a strangled sound, she quickly added, "Discreetly, of course. And I think I've got some excellent leads for you."

"Wait a minute here," Cas interrupted. "Let's get back to the part about your pumping him. What exactly did that entail?"

"We went to a bar and had a few drinks. That is, he drank, and I poured most of mine into the plastic fern next to the table." Lisel waved that part of her story aside. "The important thing is that he mentioned a few names of corporations Hinkler is involved in. He also intimated that Hinkler was very clever about setting up dummy corporations. Here . . ." She got her purse and excitedly extracted the information. "I wrote down the company names."

Cas looked at the offering in disbelief. "This is written on toilet paper!"

"That's because the ladies' room was the only place I could go to get away from Fritz." And his wandering hands, but she thought it wise not to mention that part. "Then I discovered I didn't have any paper with me."

Cas removed his glasses from his inner jacket pocket. Putting them on, he immediately looked every inch the banker—except for the toilet paper in his hands! "I'm familiar with some of these names," he murmured. "Your business contact's information seems to be pretty reliable. But this one, Contro Industries. I haven't heard that one before. May I use your phone?"

"Sure. I'm just going to go change out of these smoky clothes."

"Well, was my information useful?" Lisel questioned when she returned to the living room fifteen minutes later.

"I won't know for a few hours," Cas replied without turning around. "Meanwhile . . ." His voice ground to a halt as she came into his line of vision.

"Meanwhile?" she prompted.

"What are you wearing?" He sounded as though he were having difficulty articulating.

"This old thing?" She flicked a finger at the pure silk Prussian blue lounging outfit. Its flowing harem pants were tight at the waist and at the ankles. The top was a simple sheath cut very low and was barely held up by two delicate spaghetti straps. Over the top of the whole outfit was a diaphanous covering that shimmered with every breath she took.

Cas cleared his throat. "Is this how you vamped the information out of poor Fritz?"

"I wouldn't dream of practicing my vamp routine on anyone until I'd perfected it on you," she purred.

CHAPTER ELEVEN

Cas looked dazed but definitely entranced with the idea. "When do we start?" he demanded, his voice an eager growl.

"Right after dinner."

"How can you think of food at a time like this?" he protested.

"You'll be rewarded for your patience, don't worry." She added a teasing pat to his cheek, avoiding his retaliatory bite. "I'll just put on some music to soothe the savage beast."

The tape she chose had been designed not to soothe but to seduce. Hans had simply labeled it "ROMANTIC," and the selections included Rachmaninoff's *Rhapsody on a Theme by Paganini* and Ravel's *Bolero* as well as Elvis Presley's "Love Me Tender." Meanwhile, Lisel used the same criteria in choosing the dinner menu as she had the music. She quickly decided on stuffed mushroom caps and boiled jumbo shrimp—both fast and, more important for what she had in mind, both finger foods!

While the two dishes were cooking, Lisel called Cas into

the kitchen. "Before we can eat, we have to prepare for the feast."

Taking his hand, she led him over to the sink, where she applied a slick liquid soap from a pump dispenser to the palm of her hand. With intentional deliberation she then ran her hands over his. The soap proved to be an evocative lubricant as her fingers slid between his, loving the feel of his flesh, the sinewy strength of his fingers. Their hand-to-hand involvement soon led to mouth-to-mouth absorption in a kiss of the most passionate nature.

Lips did as hands did—merged, probed, tantalized. Lost in a wondrous haze, Lisel completely forgot her duties as chef. It took the menacing sound of a pot boiling over to bring them apart, and then only reluctantly.

"I think I'll wait for you in the living room," he muttered on a ragged breath.

By the time she carried in the trayful of goodies Cas had already set the atmosphere. A past master of the gas fireplace, he'd added light dimmers to his repertoire. His shoes lay discarded on the floor; his jacket, on the couch. But Cas himself had rejected the leather furniture in favor of the remembered softness of the alpaca rug. Lisel gracefully dropped down beside him and set the tray between them.

Lifting the first of the three covered dishes, she suggested, "Try one of these," and raised the bite-size mushroom cap to his mouth. Her fingers lingered on the firmness of his lips before reluctantly sliding away.

He returned the favor, sliding mushroom caps into her mouth with tantalizing slowness. Extra touches were added here and there, a caress to her cheek, her chin, her throat. It was amazing that they ate as much as they did, considering the continuous physical distraction each was placing on the other. Or perhaps it was the very same

172

distraction that increased the enjoyment of the food! Either way, their appetites were hearty.

Cas viewed the next course with appreciative expectation and grinned. "What's this? Sexy sushi?"

"If this were sushi, the fish would be raw." Raw was a good description of the hunger she saw in his eyes, a hunger that couldn't be satisfied with food.

This time he began, reaching in to dip a plump shrimp into the seafood dip before introducing it to her mouth. The mayonnaise-based sauce displayed a tempting tendency to cling to her lips, prompting him to kiss away the remnants. Lisel improvised her own method of dealing with the problem. When the shrimp she offered him left a wake of sauce, she swiped her index finger across his upper lip and then sucked the taste of him from her single digit.

With things progressing at this rate, it was simply a matter of time before the situation got out of hand. More kissing than eating was getting done, more earlobes than seafood being nibbled!

"Wait a minute." She placed her hand in the center of his chest, staving off a new onslaught of kissing. "There's still dessert. A favorite passion of yours."

The third, and final, cover was removed to display a bowlful of Oreo cookies. Selecting one as carefully as a connoisseur would a cigar, Lisel twisted off the top to reveal the creamy center. Lifting it to her own mouth, she used her teeth to delicately scrape the icing off the bottom half. She then transferred the cookie to Cas's mouth, so that he could do the same to the remaining icing on his section of the cookie. His teeth deliberately raked across the top of her finger, sending tiny shivers of excitement up and down her spine. Dropping the deiced cookie back to the bowl, she moved the tray aside. As a teasing prelude it had served its purpose.

173

Lisel's harem outfit and the sexual building of Ravel's *Bolero* playing on the stereo combined to inspire her for the next stage. Playing the role of a concubine, she slowly loosened Cas's tie, sliding it out from beneath the collar of his shirt, her movement synchronized to the music. Once that item of clothing had been removed, she proceeded to the buttons of his shirt, releasing each one in rhythmic succession.

For added interest, her finger introduced occasional sneak attacks beneath his now gaping shirt. The hard resilience of his chest proved to be an irresistible lure. Urging the smooth cotton shirttails free from their imprisonment within the waistband of his pants, she still managed to keep time with the gradual accentuation of the music's repetitive tempo.

His shirt now hung loosely open, inviting further exploration. Her hands surveyed the masculine terrain, mapping out erogenous zones until he captured her adventuring hands and drew one up to his mouth. There he tongue-traced each fingerprint. Lisel had no idea the tip of her finger contained so many sensory receptors. Each one vibrated with awakening sensation.

Pressing her lips against the nakedness of his chest, she let her mouth do what her captured hands couldn't. Her capricious tongue skimmed the smooth texture of his skin, tasting him in ever-increasing doses. His body could have been a magnet, so strongly did it draw her.

With a hungry groan, Cas abandoned her fingers, allowing her to slip his shirt back off his shoulders before capturing her lips for a full-dimensional kiss. In direct contrast with the hungry involvement of their mouths was the now almost tentative touch of her fingers, resting on the very tip of his bare shoulder. Unable to resist temptation for long, her fingers slid down to follow an invisible line from his Adam's apple to his navel.

174

When Cas gathered her closer, erasing the small space between them, her fingers were forced to stray to his sides, where she discovered new bone and sinew to explore. One nail provocatively rode the upward thrust of his hipbone, as she gloried in this newfound thrill of her prodigious power.

Under other circumstances Lisel might have been more than a little shocked by her own boldness. But tonight she was a mythical woman pleasing her knight in shining armor. The passage of her hands and mouth over his body was rewarded by his answering groans of pleasure.

Cas was by no means motionless while she practiced her witchcraft. Having discovered that the diaphanous covering was no more than a see-through jacket, he slipped it from her shoulders. It fell to the rug, leaving behind only the harem pants and the sheath top. His hands were now intent on stroking the silk-covered curve of her breast, his wayward caresses inciting the soft peaks to attentive rigidity.

"You're not wearing anything under this thing." He delighted in his discovery.

"*Mmm,* I know." Her voice tickled his ear.

His hand lowered to her waist and the curve of her hip. "Nothing?"

She shook her head, sending her long hair swishing out in every direction. "Not a thing."

"Oh, honey . . ." The words were breathed into her mouth as he hungrily kissed her, impelling her down onto the softness of the rug.

Now that their position had been shifted to a horizontal line, Lisel was able to feel the imprint of his body from her shoulders to her toes. His weight was a welcome burden as his thigh slid to a resting place between hers. The power of his masculinity forcefully proclaimed his need of her. Trembling from the force of her own desires, she arched against him, the movement causing an erotic friction between the tissue-soft silk of her harem pants and the already straining zipper placket of his gabardine trousers.

Coming up for air, Lisel ran her hands over the flexing muscles of his back, relishing every ridge and contour. His lips wandered across her face, closing her eyelids and teasing her lashes. The warmth of his bare chest radiated right through her thin top, burning its way to her very soul. When her hands reached the small of his back and began a daring descent, he rasped her name in primitive excitement.

The insistent shrill of the telephone sent him rolling away from her. Lisel rose to her feet in unsteady confusion, her eyes still glazed with passion as she reached for the phone. "Don't." His voice stayed her until his hand was there to do the job for him. "Don't answer it."

"It may be important," she murmured huskily.

"Nothing is more important than this." With that he swept her up in his arms.

"Where are we going?" she softly queried.

"To bed. Care to direct me?"

"But, darling," she purred in his ear, her tongue adding a provocative swirl, "I thought you didn't need a guide."

His arms tightened around her. "If you'd prefer, we can stay right here. . . ."

"No, the bedroom's up those four stairs."

Cas paused inside the bedroom door to allow her to press the light switch. "My God!" He eyed the emperor-size bed, the room's only visible furniture, in justifiable amazement. The covers had already been turned back to reveal brown satin sheets. "Your cousin does believe in doing things on a grand scale. Maybe we should go back to the living room." He teasingly turned as if to leave. "That bed's so big I might lose you in it!"

"I have no intention of letting that happen," Lisel seductively assured him.

"In that case . . ." He slowly lowered her, letting her slide along the length of his taut body as he did so. He paused when her shoulders reached the level of his mouth. "You won't need this anymore," he crooned, capturing a supporting spaghetti strap between his teeth and raking it down over the tip of her shoulder. Lisel closed her eyes in glorious ecstasy as he repeated the process on the other strap. Following the law of universal gravitation, the silken sheath slid to her waist, where his arms bound her to him.

The resultant erotic grazing of her bared, thrusting breasts against the naked planes of his chest provided a prolonged sensual assault. Their eyes were locked together as inexorably as their bodies. It was hypnotically arousing to watch the growing flames of desire flaring in his eyes. Slowly Lisel resumed her interrupted descent, her bare feet riding down the line of his shin until they came in contact with his stockinged feet. The feeling of being held aloft lasted long after her feet had touched the ground.

Lisel stood before him, proud of the unmitigated love she saw reflected on his face. The silken waterfall of her hair partially covered her pale curves, like clouds obscuring the moon. His fingers blindly searched for the fastening of her trousers, his inhaled breath a hiss of adoring disbelief when the release of one button brought about their complete downfall.

"There went the walls of Jericho!" Her husky laugh reached out to him as she scampered across the covers to perch in the middle of the bed.

Her husky laugh alone had the power to send his blood pressure soaring, but when the beauty of her nakedness was added, he was spurred to instant pursuit. In a flash he'd sprinted across the bed after her. But his fast action brought about a surprising discovery. "This is a water bed!"

"*Mmm,* that's right." She playfully nibbled on his earlobe. "Why? Do you get motion sickness?"

"Depends on what kind of motion," he cautiously replied.

"This kind." She rolled over him, entangling her legs in his.

He discarded a verbal response in favor of a much more direct physical one. Because they were caught up in the spiraling magic between them, it took them a few seconds to identify the outside source of the buzzing sound. It was her doorbell.

"Are you expecting someone?" Cas growled.

Lisel shook her head, her hair falling in a swirling curtain that surrounded them.

"Then ignore it. They'll go away."

They did go away, leaving the two lovers at peace.

"You're still wearing too many clothes," Lisel temptingly protested, reaching for his overtaxed zipper. As her fingers eased the slide fastener down its metal track, she was indelibly aware of his shuddering arousal. He raised his body as she smoothed the material down his thighs. A moment later his trousers were no longer a barrier, but a discarded article.

There was an uncontrollable urgency in the way he tumbled her from atop him, an electrifying expertise in the way his hands stoked her feminine fire. Cas was only a motion away from complete possession when he heard the unmistakable sound of the front door opening.

"Lisel, it's me!" an equally unmistakable male voice cheerfully announced.

After freezing for one stunned moment, Cas rolled away from her with a fierce oath. Blinded by frustrated fury, he grated, "This is one hell of a way to exact revenge!"

Lisel stared at him in dazed confusion. "Revenge?"

He was already off the bed, grabbing for his clothes. "What else would you call it? Settling a private account?" He rammed his legs into his trousers, refastening them with barely restrained violence. "That day in the bank you warned me, didn't you? How would you like to be left high and dry?" He furiously mimicked her. "Now I know."

Lisel didn't have the time to stay and argue with him. She could hear Hans's footsteps approaching the bedroom. Grabbing a robe from the foot of the bed, she slid into it and out the door.

She caught Hans on the bottom step of the stairs leading up to the bedroom. Seeing her, he retreated back to the living room. "What are you doing here? Why didn't you call?" she accused.

"I did call, but no one answered." Looking around at the remains of their dinner, he asked, "Did I interrupt something here?"

"No!" Thankfully the incriminating evidence of discarded articles of clothing was on the other side of the couch, out of Hans's eyesight. Her cousin wasn't called Mayer the Mouth for nothing. He had an offensive habit of using other people's embarrassments to his own advantage, deriving a perverse sort of pleasure in making situations worse. If he suspected . . .

Recovering her composure, Lisel continued in a calmer manner. "I'm just surprised to see you here, that's all." "Shocked" and "dismayed" were both actually closer to the mark.

"I got lonely for the old bachelor pad." While Hans strolled over to the aquarium, Lisel shot a nervous glance at the still-closed bedroom door.

"Edgar looks hungry," Hans complained. "I'll just go rustle up some chow for him. Has he . . ." There was a pause as he walked into the kitchen.

Consequently all Cas heard when he opened the bedroom door was the tail end of the question: ". . . been pining away with love for me, Lisel?"

Lisel gasped aloud at the open hostility displayed on Cas's face. Gone was the passionate knight of a few moments ago, and in his place was a furious, embittered man.

If Lisel thought she'd felt pain before, it was nothing compared to what she felt now with Cas looking at her with such hatred in his eyes. He didn't say a word. He just stalked down the stairs, gathered up his remaining clothing, and strode toward the apartment door. After yanking it open, he heedlessly let it slam shut behind him.

"What was all that about?" Hans inquired as he strolled back in from the kitchen.

"I love him!" Lisel whirled to shout, fed up with the way things had turned out. "And I'm going to go after him!"

Hans, looking as if he feared she might do him bodily harm, hurriedly agreed. "Sure, go after him. That sounds good." Anything to placate his obviously deranged cousin who was on her way out the door wearing only a bathrobe! "Ah, you might want to get dressed first, though," he tentatively suggested.

Lisel vehemently swore in German before pivoting and stalking back to the bedroom. In what had to be a world record, she came out again exactly seventy-five seconds later. Hans made no comment about her unusual attire, but he did insist on having Arnie call a cab for her, regardless of how nearby Cas lived. Hans also lent her his trench coat.

And so it was that Lisel arrived at Cas's building looking suspiciously like a refugee from a Halloween party. Except that Halloween wasn't for another week and a half! Her harem outfit had been the nearest article of clothing at hand, and the fastest to put on. But there was no way, by any stretch of the imagination, that her Adidas running shoes could be considered a coordinating accessory! Topped by the oversize trench coat, she felt like a misplaced flasher.

Her determination was undeterred by her peculiar physical appearance. She intended to straighten things out immediately. But despite her repeated ringing, Cas didn't answer his buzzer. She was sure he was in. It was true that he could have gone elsewhere, gone out for a drink, anything. But her instinct told her he was upstairs and ignoring the bell.

So involved was she with willing him to answer that she wasn't aware that someone had joined her in the small foyer until she heard, "Having problems?"

It was the same man who'd caught her and Cas "necking" in the freight elevator. Lisel dreaded having to turn and introduce herself, but she was desperate.

She needn't have bothered worrying. The elderly gentleman remembered her and sized up the situation pretty astutely. "You're Cas's girl, aren't you? What's wrong? Had a lovers' quarrel?"

Lisel nodded.

"Well, come on then," he said, holding open the glass security door he'd unlocked for her.

"Thank you." They entered the elevator together.

"Just name your first baby after me." The gentleman chuckled to himself.

"What's your name?" Lisel asked with a corresponding smile.

"Ezekiel Steinhelm. Don't look so dismayed, my dear." He patted her shoulder. "I was only kidding. Ezekiel Kalensky would be too much to saddle on anyone!" He tugged open the elevator door. "This is our floor. Good luck to you!"

"Thanks."

Lisel tried to disguise her knock by projecting the more masculine sound of a heavy-handed rap. She ended up with bruised knuckles, but Cas did open the door.

"What do you want?" There was no sign of welcome on his angry face.

She quickly removed her sore hand from her mouth, where she'd been nursing her knuckles. "To talk to you."

"Haven't you done enough for one night?" His eyes flashed with fury.

"Let me explain . . ."

"I'm not in any mood for explanations tonight," he dangerously noted.

"I'll take that chance," she bravely retorted.

"All right." He stood aside to let her enter. "You've got one minute."

"You've done it again, you know," she casually imparted, strolling over to his conversational pit.

"Done what?"

"Jumped to conclusions about me." She slipped off her trench coat and sat down.

"I wouldn't get too comfortable if I were you. You won't be staying."

"I believe we have to settle this little matter of a private account." She kicked off her shoes. "First off, let me say that I will strive not to hold this misunderstanding against you."

He spoke sarcastically. "How generous of you."

"I think you'll find that I can be very generous when I love someone as much as I love you."

He looked as if he'd been hit in the solar plexus. "You love me?"

"Isn't that what I just said?"

"Then why the hell didn't you tell me?"

She pretended to pout. "You're not going to get angry all over again, are you?"

182

"No, I'm not." He sat down next to her on the couch and enfolded her in his arms. "I love you." His words were murmured against the vulnerable pulse at her temple. "You really *do* believe in us?"

"I love you. I'd hardly have braved coming here if I didn't." She nuzzled his throat. "I never planned on being interrupted like that. It was as painful and as frustrating for me as it was for you."

"Who was that guy?" Cas leaned away to growl.

"My cousin Hans."

"Mayer the Mouth?"

Lisel wryly nodded. "The one and the same." Returning to his embrace, she said, "Now, if you don't mind, I think we have some unfinished business to transact."

He dropped a brief but heady kiss on her parted lips. "First I've got something to show you."

"I can hardly wait." Her seductive expression was marred by a frown at his withdrawal.

"Close your eyes and put out your hands," he instructed.

She did so.

"Okay, now open." She parted her lips, certain this ruse must be the prelude to some romantic love scene.

"No, open your eyes," he clarified.

"Chocolate." She looked at the giant-size Hershey's kiss he had placed in her outstretched hands. "How nice. But I seem to have an insatiable hunger for something else at the moment."

"Unwrap this first."

"Cas . . ." Lisel was beginning to despair of ever picking up where they'd left off!

"The sooner you do this," he tempted her, "the sooner we can complete our transactions."

"Well, since you put it like that."

"I thought you'd see things my way."

183

"You know, this feels awfully light," she commented while removing the foil wrapping.

"That may be because the center is hollowed out."

"Hollowed out? Why?"

He cast her a teasing grin. "Look and ye shall see."

She lifted the top off the chocolate kiss and exclaimed, "There's a box in here!"

"There certainly is."

Opening the jeweler's box, she huskily asked, "Does this mean what I think it does?" Unknowingly she'd repeated the very question he'd asked her the night they'd made love in the Alps.

Taking his cue from her, he confirmed it, saying "I guess it does," just as she had that night. After lifting the aquamarine engagement ring from its velvet bed, he reached for her left hand and slid the ring onto the proper finger. "That makes it official." He retained his hold on her hand, lifting it for her appraisal. "Do you like it?"

"I love it, but it looks terribly expensive."

"That's all right." He waved her concern aside. "I've just gotten promoted for nabbing Hinkler."

"You nabbed Hinkler! In the past half hour?"

"Well, not exactly nabbed," he modestly admitted. "But I thought the term appropriate in light of your own undercover operations."

"Did I help?"

"You cracked the case. One of the companies you gave me on that biodegradable list, Contro Industries, was the vital missing link between Hinkler and a scam involving that dummy corporation in Brazil. He'd pulled the same stunt there, requesting and receiving a loan to build a factory. But the factory was never built because Hinkler slipped out of the country with all the money. I finished talking to my contact right before you came knocking on

184

my door. That's why I didn't answer my buzzer. I was on the phone, and the call was long distance."

"What will happen to him now?"

"He won't get a loan from our bank or from any other financial institution checking his credit record here in the States. The federal authorities are also interested in speaking to Herr Hinkler. But enough about him. Are you sure you like your ring? I thought you might prefer a diamond, but this reminded me of the color of the Alpine lakes you loved so much."

"I'm positive." She leaned forward to kiss him. "I love it!"

"Good. Now that that's settled, we only have one more thing to cover."

Her finger insinuated itself between the buttons of his shirt, straying inside to tease his bare skin with her nail. "I was thinking more in the lines of *un*covering."

"First I want to apologize—"

Lisel covered his mouth with her hand. "Apology accepted. Accounts settled. Now, if we could get on to the next matter at hand. Oh!"

Lisel's abrupt inhalation was caused by his bold removal of her top. He tossed it over his shoulder with a cavalier devilment she found contagious. Her fingers made short work of the buttons on his shirt, and it was efficiently stripped and tossed over *her* shoulder. The few remaining items of their clothing were soon strewn over the floor with casual disregard for neatness. The time for playful teasing and tempting foreplay was done.

With no barriers left between them, their passions flared quickly out of control. An electrifying thrust of his hips made her his, coupling them together for the most intimate of journeys. His slow, driving rhythm excited her to ragged moans.

Their lovemaking held all the climactic energy of ther-

185

mal fusion. The tension built to unbearable levels as they hovered on the spire of desire. One final shuddering propulsion resulted in their simultaneous release. Cas's satisfaction was shouted against the arching warmth of her neck as Lisel held him to her, surrendering to the perpetual motion coursing through her.

Sometime later that night, after they'd both retired to his bed, she was unable to resist murmuring, "No more second thoughts?"

His hands continued their leisurely stroll around her curves. "Plenty. And third and fourth thoughts as well. All of which revolve around you."

"Care to elaborate?"

His caresses instantly became daringly intimate as he enthusiastically accepted her invitation. "I'd love to!"

LOOK FOR NEXT MONTH'S
CANDLELIGHT ECSTASY ROMANCES ®:

All-new
Candlelight
Newsletter

**An exceptional,
free offer awaits readers
of Dell's incomparable Candlelight Ecstasy and Supreme Romances.**

Subscribe to our all-new CANDLELIGHT NEWSLETTER and you will receive—at absolutely no cost to you—exciting, exclusive information about today's finest romance novels and novelists. You'll be part of a select group to receive sneak previews of upcoming Candlelight Romances, well in advance of publication.

You'll also go behind the scenes to "meet" our Ecstasy and Supreme authors, learning firsthand where they get their ideas and how they made it to the top. News of author appearances and events will be detailed, as well. And contributions from the Candlelight editor will give you the inside scoop on how she makes her decisions about what to publish—and how *you* can try your hand at writing an Ecstasy or Supreme.

You'll find all this and more in Dell's CANDLELIGHT NEWSLETTER. And best of all, *it costs you nothing*. That's right! It's Dell's way of thanking our loyal Candlelight readers and of adding another dimension to your reading enjoyment.

Just fill out the coupon below, return it to us, and look forward to receiving the first of many CANDLELIGHT NEWSLETTERS—overflowing with the kind of excitement that only enhances our romances!

Return to: DELL PUBLISHING CO., INC.   B251A
        Candlelight Newsletter • Publicity Department
        245 East 47 Street • New York, N.Y. 10017

Name_____

Address_____

City_____

State_____Zip_____

Candlelight Ecstasy Romances™

$1.95 each

Candlelight
Ecstasy Romances™

Candlelight
Ecstasy Romances™

$1.95 each

At your local bookstore or use this handy coupon for ordering:

DELL BOOKS
P.O. BOX 1000. PINE BROOK. N.J. 07058-1000   B251D

Please send me the books I have checked above. I am enclosing $ _____ (please add 75c per copy to
cover postage and handling). Send check or money order—no cash or C.O.D.'s. Please allow up to 8 weeks for
shipment.

Name _____

Address _____

City _____ State Zip _____